Those Who Inherit the Will of the Damned

Those Who Inherit the Will of the Damned

Daniel Brown

To order additional copies of this book, contact:
Xlibris Corporation
1-888-795-4274
www.Xlibris.com
Orders@Xlibris.com
37276

For:

Mom, Dad, Ali, and everyone in my family.
Also, for Andrea, Eric, Ricardo, Kelsey, Kristen, Jon, Steve, Ed, Tommy, Stan,Chris and everyone else who I forgot to mention from Karate or S&T. You all are the best friends ever (it's the truth!).

Also, thanks to any I forgot to mention who've helped me through my so called Life. Teachers, Guidance Counselors, Significant others . . . all them folks.

****1****

Daima nursed the mug in his hand, listening to the song, as it ebbed and flowed like the tides of the great seas. The girl who sung it was talented, if the song didn't strike a chord in him. Several rather drunk men were looking lustfully at her, and he had to resist the urge to snarl at them. Best not to reveal his other side, if he could help it.

> "*Oh, the dawn follows the birds, and I cry,*
> *I cry for all those lost to me,*
> *Dawn casts its fingers o'er the battlefield,*
> *And, I know, with dread e'er in my heart,*
> *That my life, my love, is lost to me,*
> *E'er I cry for my loss, I strive to live on,*
> *And remember, always to remember,*
> *For those we lost, for those we found,*
> *And never forget the diligent few, of*
> *Those we buried in the Mourning Grounds,*
> *And, if you should say to forget,*
> *Then I will tell thee true,*
> *I will continue waiting.*

There were several more verses to the song, but Daima tuned them out when he heard Nainya start to growl in his mind. Either he didn't like the subject of the song, or something bad was happening. Or both. As it turned out, it was both.

A drunken man stumbled toward the girl, hand reaching out toward her dress, which hung loosely about her knees. "Hey, gurlie, washamatta, hah? C'mon, lesh you'n me go an' 'play' a bit, yesh? Get over hersh, damnit!" He made a lunge, and the girl screamed, hands flying up to her face, closing her eyes. For a moment, there was silence.

When she opened her eyes, the man was lying on the ground, coughing slightly, gazing dazedly at the man standing in front of him. His eyes glared down at the rowdy drunkard, who managed to realize that he was outmatched here. A scar ran jaggedly down his face.

Everyone stared at the stranger, who wore a simple cloak and jerkin, his boots looking well worn from his travels. His hair fell to his shoulders, barely, strong and black in color. No one said a word, and he turned to leave. Then, the spell was broken, and everyone started talking again, all at once. The girl rushed out after him, calling, "Wait, wait!"

He stopped a moment, turning to her slightly. "Yes?" It was the first time he had spoken, and his voice was deep, almost a growl.

"Uh, I . . . I wanted to know how I could thank you, for . . . for that . . ."

"What, the drunk? If you want to repay me, then learn to defend yourself. The time is past for damsels in distress, and if you don't realize that soon, then you'll find that no one is really waiting to defend you from whatever's out there. Get me?"

"Uh, uh-huh!" The poor girl had wide eyes, starting at him. He supposed he may have gone a bit hard on her, but he had learned the hard way that it was a hard world. She would be better off, in the end. He hoped.

There was a soft rustling from the side of the road where they stood. All that was here was an inn and stables for traveler's horses. So, no garrison, which was why he had chosen it. Now, he was starting to realize the downside of that. Within his head, he heard Nainya growl. He was on edge, and his nerves had saved them both more than a few times, in the war and the Hunt. Too bad, they weren't suited to that, they usually were the hunters. He turned to her. "Get inside. Now."

"But—"

"I said NOW!!!" He practically roared it, and she screamed, covering her head as she scampered back inside. But he hadn't scared her.

He turned quickly, rolling to his left as the clawed hand of the creature took a swipe at his head, barely missing his skull. He got out of the roll, reaching for his sword. Problem was, it was still in his room, as weapons weren't allowed in the common room. Damn.

He got a good look at the thing. It had little tufts of hair all over its body, and it stood upright, looking at him. Its claws had dried blood on them. But it was its eyes that Daima found the worst. Those eyes, they were . . . almost human. Tortured and driven by nothing more than rage and hate, piercing yellow with a small crescent in each . . . but human nonetheless. A were-bear. This could well have been a comrade of his, during the war.

A lot of Naish had gone insane, upon the King's betrayal to the entire race. They could no longer control the urges that their feral sides gave them, and their already fragile minds had shattered from the strain. They had mutated into something neither animal nor human. An abomination.

He had only one thing to do that may cause him to live after this. It was suicidal and almost certainly not going to work. Ah, the threat of a painful death was the spice of life for him and Nainya. He dived straight at the beast, catching it off guard. As it took a swipe at the man, it was surprised to find that the man had changed into a black wolf, fur as pitch black as pure dark. And teeth that were soon tainted red with the blood of this innocent. Gore worked its way into its once uncontaminated coat, and Nainya shivered. Quickly, he changed back to Daima, going transparent for but a moment.

When everyone rushed out side, as usual a few moments too late, all they found was a beast, its throat ripped out, and a man, a feral grimace on his face as he pushed by the gawking spectators.

It was no longer safe here; he had revealed the half of him that would do best to stay out of the public eye. And what a pity, he had so wanted to have a real bed to sleep on tonight, before he made his way back to the Sentinels.

He felt Nainya whimper an apology to him, but he shook it off. *'No need, old chum. I've learned not to keep my hopes up too much. And, it's not like another night in the wild will kill me'*. He felt the wolf reside, a little.

He grabbed his pack, which now felt pitifully light from sixth month's hard travel. He shrugged it on, and grabbed his sword, Sapanh. He had picked it up in Aviary from one of the resident elves there, whose name he couldn't rightly remember now. Her'lind'uliya, or something like that. Either which way, the runes he had put into it were protection against more spells than either man or wolf knew, and they knew quite a few between them.

With his sword at his hip, loosened incase the inn's patrons decided to turn violent, he stalked down the stairwell into the common room.

A dozen pairs of glaring eyes met him, killing intent literally dripping off of them. Luckily, no one decided to do anything about it. He didn't mind the evil stares. He had lived with them long enough.

It was almost funny, how so quickly the people of Hring, Dunland, Pasival, and the other parts of the Empire had turned on the Naish and the Elves and the Dwarves. In the course of two days, they had gone from returning victorious heroes to something akin to monsters. So, they had obliged them in return.

They wanted monsters, and that's what they got.

The night was dark and cold. But not as cold as Daima Ulu'Daen's heart. He had killed it a long time ago. His eyes were merely cold chips of ice, hard and sharp and deadly. Or, at least, that is what he wished them all to believe. It was harder to work up the courage to kill something if you knew that it would kill you first with nary a second thought

The girl he had saved peeked her head out shyly from the doorway. *No*, he told himself, *not a girl. She is a woman, with a woman's stubbornness, if not a woman's prudence.* He turned to her slightly, letting his scabbard show true to her. "Yes?"

"You . . . your one of . . . of them?" She sounded timid. Probably was, when it came right down to it, but he couldn't really blame her. She was out of her league here.

He sighed. Oh, great, another friendship shattered . . . well, *potential* friendship. "Yes. If you wish to try anything, please don't bother. I know my way around a blade better than anyone in there, so I seriously doubt that you have a chance against me. And . . . I do not wish to hurt you."

She seemed taken aback, as if the prospect hadn't even crossed her mind. That meant that she was either innocent or incredibly stupid, or both. And, she didn't seem to be the stupid type, so he opted to believe that she was simply innocent. "O-oh! No, I . . . I wanted to come with you! Y-you said that I should learn to defend myself better, and what better way than with a Naish?"

He sighed, shaking his head. "No, no you can't." He fought down a wince at the hurt look on her face. She could barely be sixteen, to his thirty. This would be awkward, even if he could convince her not to come. "Sorry, but it's just too dangerous. Mine is a hard life, and filled with things that you haven't even seen in a nightmare. Well, not yet. You may not realize it, but your so-called *beloved King* is really doing a piss-poor job of defending the borderlands, more concerned with eradicating the Elves, Dwarves, and the Naish." A sad look crossed his face. "Either way, I can't let you come. Go home, girl."

"Brenna."

"What?"

"My name . . . is Brenna Turlin."

He stood stock still for a moment. Turlin . . . Turlin . . . could this be her daughter? "And I am called Daima. Girl . . . Brenna . . . who was your mother?"

"What?"

He sighed. Okay, so maybe she wasn't entirely innocent. "You're *Mother*. You know, the one who birthed you, raised you, taught you how to live?"

"Oh . . . oh . . ." a look of pained sadness crossed her face. "I . . . never had one. She . . . she left me here when I was only little. People here . . . they said she was very beautiful . . . said that I should be proud to be her daughter . . . but . . . I never knew her . . ."

"I'm sorry, Brenna."

She sniffed one last time, wiping her eyes with her jacket sleeve. "Don't be. I got over it a long time ago."

"You have no idea," he muttered absentmindedly to himself.

"What?"

"Huh? Oh, nothing. Listen, Brenna . . ." he took a deep breath to steady himself. "Go home. Wherever that is. What you want I cannot, nor will not give. It would destroy you."

"What . . . what would?"

"Brenna . . . everyone has a beast inside of them. For people like me, it just has a name."

"People . . . like . . . you?" She looked very confused, and had every right to be.

"Your mother . . . I knew her . . ."

"'Knew her' . . . like—"

"NO!!! Not like that," he finished hastily. "Your Mother . . . she was an Elf. And, more than that, she was a Naish, though I never met her other half. So, for the betterment of both of us, just forget that I was ever here. Never tell anyone of this secret, for they will alienate you and kill you for being this."

"But, WHY? Why do they fear us because we are different?" Her tone was now sullen and a little angry. Amazing how fast opinions could change when the person on the outside went from being someone else to being you.

"Why?" He asked in a sneering tone. "Why? Because they don't know how to deal with someone who isn't conformed to what they are or what they think is 'normal' and 'natural'. If it were up to the King of men, then there would be no more magic in the world, only his industry and fire and foul abominations," he said wryly. "They . . . are afraid of us. Or, rather, of me. They don't understand me, so they question my right to live among them. Bloody prigs."

She gave a little laugh of the use of a Dunlandish curse; she had only heard a few others in the inn. Then, her expression hardened. "Daima . . . who . . . who was my Mother?"

He sighed. He had known that this was coming, but had vainly hoped she would drop it. "Your mother . . . she was very beautiful. Graceful, and strong and proud, and she was a mage of the Naish. Her name was Lilain'Turlin'Kial. She was not only powerful in magic, but strong in use of both blade and bow. That was why it was such a shock when she was killed."

"By who? If she was so powerful, then how was she felled? Why did she leave me as something other than her own child?"

Daima knew he had to make this quick. It was a Hunter's moon tonight, and he wanted to go before the locals got a chance to skewer him with various sharp and pointy things that should do well to be not sticking out of his hide. "As for the first question, her name was Alaia' Turlin' Laen, she left you here before she left with me and a few of us who still had the will to fight. She was felled in the Battle of The Bistairne River. There were thousands of the King's Soldiers, against only a couple hundred of us."

"'Us', as in . . . ?"

"Naish, Elves, Dwarves, and a few free men who decided they'd rather have some mystery and magic in the world than simply pure science. And, this was before the beasts of Wold decided to help out." He shook his head, unconsciously releasing a low growl from the back of his throat which made the frightened girl take a step back. "We slaughtered them, and yet still they kept coming. We rained down Mage Fire on them until our mages had nigh on killed themselves, and still they could not ford the River against us. We barricaded the far side with the bodies of the slain to stop the cavalry charges. We knocked them into the River so that they drowned in their heavy armor. But, there were so many, and they took each of us slain as solace for their losses, even if it was two score for every one of us that fell in battle. Me, your mother, Gamling, Asteroth, and maybe a dozen others kept to the defense of the bridge, even as we knew all was lost. Then, your Mother turned to me. She and another High Elf, Telin'adun'Laen, they bid us away with all haste. They would hear no argument against them. Those few of us left, maybe three score, we fled back in this direction. After a few minutes, there was a flash, and when we came back, there was no more bridge. But, the River was damned with the bodies of the King's men. At least two thousand of them!"

Her eyes showed her shock true, and she gasped slightly. "A-and . . . why did she . . . who was . . . my father?"

"I can only guess, but I assume that he was a man, otherwise your ears would have pointed long before now."

"So . . . I am . . . a half-breed?"

"If you wish to call yourself that, but most among us would say a Half-Elf. They are rare, as Elves of either sex will rarely take a human lover. Consider yourself lucky that your father earned such an honor, otherwise you most surely would be dead by now."

"I see . . . so, I'll go get my things."

"No, you shall not. You will stay where it is safe, you have maybe half a year or so before your ears start pointing. Take that blessing for what it is, and good luck. I am off. Goodbye, Brenna Turlin . . . Brenn a'Adun'Kial." He turned away from her, having wasted more time than he should have. He started towards the trees that marked the edge of the forest that industry had yet to claim as its fuel, allowing Nainya out. The wolf inside of him, his Bond-Brother, was black as the night, with piercing yellow eyes with a small crescent in each, marking him as Naish. He was transparent for but a moment before he was out of Daima and into the world.

One of the reasons that Humans feared the Naish was the idea of two souls sharing a body, thinking of the spree of possessions that had plagued the populace during the War. In actuality, it was more like a dream, and a rather nice one at that. It was nice to be able to kick back and let someone else do everything for a change, eating, walking, fighting, and the like. When Daima Receded, he found himself in a very nice inn, much better than the one they had just frequented, and he and several Dwarves were drinking heavily. Dwarves were the best drinking partners, as they always were the types to get "Happy" drunk instead of "Violent/ Suicidal/ Psychopathic" drunks that many humans became (if they didn't pass out first). Of course, it hadn't been like that before or even during the War, but alcohol always made him feel better, even if he had to suffer a hangover afterwards (but, in the Dreamland, hangovers were just a figment of his imagination).

He had no idea what Nainya's Dreamland was like, but he suspected it had something to do with trees. Lots and lots of trees.

2

Nainya padded through the forest, periodically stopping to sniff the clean air there. But, he wasn't doing it for his health. It was because that something was wrong. An unfamiliar scent. That was almost never good, in his long lived experience (for a wolf). But, there was another scent on the air, slightly more familiar, but he couldn't place it.

Suddenly, he picked up the pungent tang of a fox. It was unmistakable; the red little beasts couldn't hide from a wolf, or at least not for long. And, any fox or kitsune below a six-tails was automatically below any wolf alpha. Sure enough, he could soon see the fox . . . no, fox *spirit.* The kitsune had seven tails sticking out where there should naturally only be one . . . but nature had taken a breather on the logic part when she had created foxes. The little blighters could even escape death, immediately becoming fox spirits, the kitsune. As they gained in experience and (hopefully) wisdom, they gained tails. Each tail meant more respect and social standing among the twelve Celestial Beasts and all animals in general.

Nainya came up to it in full view, and the spirit immediately bared its neck to him as a sign of respect, although she needn't have done so to him, as they were equals. Any fox can smell a wolf who is an alpha male; it is distinctly different from the scent of any other wolf.

Although most Wolves and Foxes could not speak in human languages, theirs was a tongue of growls and yips and the like. Daima had a grasp on it, although his mouth could not form but rudimentary words, so he stuck to man-speech. The kitsune flared her tails in warning.

'Honored Leader, there is someone coming behind you, a Human Girl, around sixteen years of age, by her scent. She is pungent with the odor of Hunters!'

'Thank you, Friend, but we know of this child. It appears that she is a fool who does not know how to take any orders from her betters. We shall let her find us, and shall reprimand her for her trespass. But, I know that you would not come for but a warning that any self-respecting wolf or fox could smell from a mile off. What is your mission, friend?'

The kitsune gave a small bow to the Wolf, front limbs splayed out gracefully. 'I thank you, and you are correct. I am to inform you and your bond Brother, there is a mighty gathering of the Forest, the Wolves and the Foxes and the Boars and all our allies, the Elves and Dwarves and the like. Runners have been sent to find any Naish that yet still walk among us as whole of mind and spirit. It shall take place in about two suns from here, to the North and a little East, through the Forest.'

Nainya, being courteous as he was, bowed back to the Fox spirit. 'I, we, thank you, friend Spirit. May your Tails grow both many and beautiful!' Of course, this is the polite way to end a conversation between beasts, an exchanging of compliments.

'I thank you. May your coat never falter, and may it shine for ever!' The Kitsune vanished in a burst of fire, although there was no smoke at all. A Kitsune can control both fire and themselves, although they preferred to show off their tails. But, they could take the form of a human, depending on their gender. For a man to gain the favor of a Kitsune was a sign of good luck and fortune.

Nainya sat down, resting his head on his paws, and waited for Brenna. The girl may be clumsy and stink of Humans and their foul drinks, but she was an adept enough tracker that she would find them soon enough.

Until then, he would take a nap in the sunlight.

She was softly singing to herself, some half-remembered tune that she somehow managed to keep in her head long enough to sing the words.

"We move in light and love,
We pray to Gods above,
And we know, that,
We are not alone,
We feel an unseen love,
We are the loved of a Light above,
And we are His children here.

We are to be found by our Truths,
We are to find our path.
We are to be unmatched.
White death sheds the black night,
Leagues from lightning flash,
Scrape your skin, guard your soul,
Roll your heart in ash,
Save yourself and Hold Fast, Hold—"

There was a flash of fire next to her, and she cried out and held up her fists in some mockery of a fighting stance, ready to defend herself however she could. But, all there was next to her was a fox.

She sighed, giving it a grin. "Oh, dear, Fox, you scared me there. I had feared for my life!"

"Well, you shouldn't have! I would not hurt you unless you had threatened me or my kits. Well, if I had any, that is."

"What? Are . . . you . . . *talking*?"

"Why, of course, dear! I am a Kitsune, and we gain the Gift of Tongues after our sixth tail, and, as you can see, I have seven!" She turned about, showcasing her tails, which shimmered with an inner fire all their own. Truly, a Kitsune was not a beast to be crossed lightly. The Fox-spirit looked her over. She wore a brown jacket and tight pants, also a dull brown. A cap was nestled on her head, reaching the tops of her ears. Her hair hung down in a pony-tail to the middle of her shoulders.

Brenna stared at the she-Fox spirit. The Kitsune gave her an innocent look. "What?"

The girl shook her head to clear it. "Oh, right, um . . . you say you're a Kitsune?"

The Fox chuckled a little. "Well, let's see . . . I died, I have seven tails, I travel with the help of my inner fires . . . yep, I am most definitely a Kitsune."

"I was always told that they . . . that you . . . were just a myth, like the Forest Gods."

Her eyes slanted a bit, giving her a fierce visage that made Brenna involuntarily take a step back. "No, I *am* real. And, so are the Forest Protectors. Just because you humans wish things away and ignore them does not make them go away. Your will is misplaced, as is your faith in your Industry's. The fire that melts steel can not match my own, and mine can not match Brithal's."

"Brithal?"

The seven-Tails sighed. "Brithal, dear heart, is the majestic ruler of all Foxes and Kitsune. He is made of a pure flame, and he has sixty-four shining, fiery tails. And his eyes . . ." The Fox spirit sighed happily; letting images of her leader come up.

Brenna gave her a confused look. The Kitsune, realizing that she had been day-dreaming, shook her head, as if to shake of a fly there. Brenna laughed softly. "Well, I guess I have to believe you. After all, I have met one of the Naish, a Kitsune, and, apparently, am a Half-Elf." The seven-Tailed Fox cocked her head to one side, doing her best to give a quizzical expression through her red fur. "What?"

"A Half-Elf, you say? What is your name, girl?"

"Brenna."

"Your full name, your *real* name!" The Fox was a bit snappish at her.

"Uh, Daima told me yesterday . . . Brenna'Adun'Kial."

"Hmmm . . . interesting."

"How, exactly?"

"Oh? I knew your mother, she was a good Elf. Very powerful in her own right, even without Fafhrir."

"Who?"

"Her Bond-Brother. He was a mighty Dragon, an heir to the line of Fafnir, if I'm not mistaken, even though I don't know how."

"Who's Fafnir?"

The Kitsune shook her head bemusedly. "Oh, boy, you Humans sure know how to dumb down your kits . . . Fafnir is the mighty Lady of all Dragons, and the Arch-Rival of Graechin, Lord of the Wyrms."

"Wyrm? What's a Wyrm? Because I get the feeling you're not talking about those squiggly things that birds eat."

"And you'd be right! A Wyrm is a lot like a Dragon, except that they can not breathe fire and they are much, much stronger physically than any Dragon under a thousand years of age."

Brenna whistled softly. "Well! But, what are you really doing here? And what is your name? I have given you mine, and it is common courtesy to give me yours."

The Fox-spirit laughed a small, light laugh. *'Oh, this one is not as dense as her ancestry would provide. Oh, it is good to welcome in new blood!'* The Kitsune laughed again. "I am called Reytha. It is Elvish for 'Swift-Footed'. I like it well enough."

"Hmmm . . . so do I . . . Reytha. Now, do you know where Daima the Naish is?"

"Why, yes! In fact, he is expecting you."

"Oh! Well, let's go already!"

She walked towards the Kitsune, who immediately got up from the log she had been resting upon. Reytha started off into the dawning Forest, Brenna following.

Daima rested lightly against the tree that Nainya had recently been resting in front of. The Wolf had informed him of the Kitsune and Brenna, and he was now in the Dreamland, doing whatever he wanted. The Forest was just awakening, bird-song lightly breaking the silence as sun broke through the tree cover. He was content to just sit and wait for the girl.

The Kitsune was a different matter entirely. While never outright evil, they *were* still foxes at heart, no matter how many tails they grew, and as such were mischievous pranksters. Also, a Fox was a master at tactics, due to the pranks they made it their life's mission to pull off, each one more spectacular than the last. If she really wanted, she could get Brenna lost in the Forest and make him go after her. But, he hoped that the summons from Lord Brithal would stay her pranks . . . for the moment.

While outwardly calm, he was tense on the inside. His sense of smell was better than most human's (thanks to the fact that there was a rather large wolf inside of him), so he smelled the two long before he heard them. The Kitsune gave off an unmistakable smell, and the girl smelled of the inn, whose stench was a pungent scar on the normally fragrant forest. Sure enough, the padding of pawed feet, followed by the soft footfalls of a pair of shoes.

The Kitsune hove into view first, followed almost immediately by Brenna. The girl seemed a little dazed, but he couldn't blame her in the least. This was a bit much to take in, in such a small amount of time.

He stood and bowed to the Fox Spirit, then turned to Brenna. "So . . . I take it you didn't bother listening to me?"

She looked at the ground guiltily. "N . . . no . . . I . . . well . . . see!" She abruptly ripped the cap from her brown-topped head, revealing the very tops of her ears. They tapered to a slight point, showing her Elven blood true to them. At the same time, she pulled up her sleeve, revealing a long, nasty bruise there.

Daima took a step closer, looking at her quizzically. "What happened? Did these grow in last night? And who did this to you"

She didn't stop looking at the ground. "They just appeared this morning . . . I don't know what to do! My friends . . . they won't take me back in now! When the cleaning lady saw me, she screamed and threw a bar stool at me! I'm . . . I'm just a freak!!!" Tears started slowly dripping their way down her face, digging furrows there.

Daima gently took her face in one of his hands. "No . . . you are what you will yourself to be. Just because your ears gained a point overnight does not mean the end of the world for you . . . in fact . . . think of it as a new beginning."

"You're just saying that," she sniffed.

He grinned. "Is it helping?"

She couldn't help but laugh a little. "Yeah, a bit . . . but, where can I go now?"

He sighed, and his shoulders slumped a little. "Well . . . I guess I have no choice but to take you to the Resistance, they can—"

"Wait . . . your saying that the group that is trying to topple the Empire, a group of mages and Elves and Dwarves and Naish and animals . . . and the best name you could come up with is 'The Resistance'?"

"Yeah, why?"

"Shouldn't it be . . . I dunno, something a little bit flashier?"

"So what? The Elves have a name for it, but no one really uses it in passing."

"What is it?"

"Poden-ret-hyu'ni-taffa-gyun-killadsamanah."

"Oh . . . so, 'The Resistance' it is, then!"

"Yes. So, off we go . . ."

She smiled and put her cap back on. He saw this, and said, "Don't do that. Bare pride for what you are and what you maybe. You are a Half-Elf, and you also have Dragon Tamer's blood in you, from your mother. Never disgrace her memory by covering up your ears, unless you must. While traveling, let them stay out. You'll feel better for it."

Indeed, her head felt clearer and quicker when she didn't have her cap on. She stashed it in her pocket. She followed him off, until the Kitsune stepped in front of them.

"Why, Daima, I'm surprised at you! Don't you give your old friend even a greeting?"

"'Old Friend'? I don't even know you!"

The Fox chuckled. "Oh, I think you do. Just a moment . . ." She spun around very quickly, and a cyclone of fire surrounded her. When it cleared, a woman stood there, with silver hair, and an outfit similar to Brenna's on, except that it was green. But the most startling thing about her was the fact that seven fiery red tails splayed themselves out behind her, flicking this way and that in defiance of the wind.

As soon as he saw this, Daima rushed up and hugged her. "Reytha! I had thought you might have perished long ago, what with the King's campaign striking so close to home! Good to see you, old friend. But, how come I or Nainya did not smell you?"

She smiled, revealing pearly whites that shone in the dim Forest light. "I wear perfume when I'm human, silly, not when I'm a Fox! You just got used to that scent, and not my natural one, is all!"

"Ah, that explains it. When did you get your tail? When we last saw you, what was it, three years back? Yes, that was it, well, as I recall, you only had six tails."

"Oh, I got this not three weeks after I last saw you. Fought an ogre to a standstill, yes I did. The old brute was praying on a Hunter's village, and the poor people there were getting raided almost every night! He retreated, and I managed to find his lair, with him in it. Finished him off with a blast of Fire, and led some of the men back there to get all their things back. Soon as we started celebrating, I began growing it in, and it came in later that night. No as painful as the last, I tell you true!"

Brenna gently touched Daima's shoulder. "Ummm, excuse me, but I'm kind of lost. What's all this about Tails and such?"

Reytha spoke up. "You see, dear, a Kitsune gains tails when they do great deeds and such. As I can recall, there have only been two nine-tails, which is the largest amount of tails any regular Kitsune can reach. Brithal has sixty-four, but he is a God, after all. But, there have been some two dozen eight-tails running about . . ." The Fox-Woman trailed off into thought. Almost as an afterthought, she reached over and placed her hand on the place where Brenna's bruise was. A white light surrounded it, and when Brenna moved her sleeve up again, it was gone entirely.

"Whoa . . . thanks! But, why haven't there been more? Is the task you have to do stupendously hard or something?"

The Seven-tails laughed. "Oh, no, no, no! Not at all, it is set as more a personal goal than anything else. No cosmic force tells us what to do, so we just do we simply do what we think is best for everyone. In reality, only we can choose whether we can be a Nine Tails or not . . . but it is more than just facing your fears. It is finding them, embracing them, and learning to live with them."

"Oh. Wait . . . you're a *Kitsune*, and a seven-tails at that . . . what on Earth do you fear?"

Reytha smiled sadly. "That's the problem . . . I've faced death too many times to be bothered by it now, let alone fear it . . . it is what is within myself that I fear, and facing it may destroy me. But, all that in its own time, yeah?"

Brenna nodded. Reytha smiled all the while, and said, "C'mon, you two! I can lead you there . . . but, you should have a weapon of some sort, Dear. The Forest can be a dangerous place for humans, after all, even if they're a Half-Elf like you. Just a moment!" She spun around, and another cyclone of Blue-tinged flame engulfed her. When it cleared, she was gone.

"Where'd she go?" Brenna rushed over to where the Kitsune had just stood; leaving only a little bit of scorched earth where she had been. Daima put his hand on her shoulder in a comforting way.

"Don't worry; she just went to get you a weapon, is all. She'll be back in a little bit, don't worry. Just relax a bit, okay? Worrying never did a body much good, and what little that was is sure not noticeable in the bad it does. Sit down, take a nap. Reytha is safe, I've seen her go through Hell and back with not a scratch on her."

Slowly, the tense girl relaxed, a little. At least it was a start. Daima leaned back against a log, letting his eyes close halfway, watching the young woman. She fidgeted about, playing with her hands to distract herself.

True to her word, five minutes later Reytha appeared, right next to Brenna. The poor girl, who had been dozing a little, nearly jumped straight out of her skin with fear. Instead, she settled for jumping up and tripping over a log. Reytha gave a full throated laugh, and Daima had tears of mirth in his eyes. Nainya howled his approval, although only his Bond-brother could hear it. Brenna looked up icily at the Fox-woman, who carried a bow and a quiver of arrows. "Reytha, you're horrible! I was worried about you, and you scare me half to death!"

Daima wiped some tears from his eyes. "Maybe, but your face was *priceless*! And, give her a break! She's a Kitsune, pranks and such are in her blood and brain!"

"He's right, dear. Sorry if I scared you, but I couldn't resist. Either way, there is a change of plans. Meeting place has been changed, from Bestiary to Aviary."

All mirth left his form as Daima groaned. "Oh, damn it all! So, the High and Mighty decides to put all us land-walkers through Hell, eh?"

"Pretty much. But, I do have Brenna's weapon. Here you are, dear," said Reytha, handing Brenna the yew bow and oak arrows, around two dozen in all, and all of them fletched with strange green feathers.

She cautiously took them, and tested out the pull of the string, and finding it satisfactory. She slung the quiver over her shoulder. "What bird has green feathers?"

"That's the feathers of a molted phoenix, they are! Best thing for arrows, if a bit hard to come by." The Kitsune seemed overly proud of herself for this.

"Have a go, then! Try to hit the knot in that tree," said Daima, pointing to a tree around sixty yards hence. A knot, maybe a hand span wide and long lay in the center of it, looking only a slight discoloration against the drab brown of the tree's bark. Brenna gave him a look that clearly said, *'Go and die you prick'*. Either way, she took out an arrow and sighted down the shaft. With a quick release of the end of the thing, she let fly. It sped quickly towards her target, and made contact just above the middle exact of the knot in the bole of the tree. She smiled slightly, while Daima whistled and Reytha clapped lightly in appreciation.

"Did a lot better than *I* ever could," said Daima to Reytha. The Kitsune nodded in agreement as Brenna went and took the arrow from the tree with a little bit of effort. She smiled cutely, eliciting a scowl from Daima. She simply put the arrow back and unstrung her bow. She slung it over her shoulder, holding it by the now lank string.

Reytha motioned to her. "Come on, Love, we must be going! The meeting at Aviary is starting in a few days, so we need to hurry if we wish to get there on time!"

"But, why can't you just do that thing with the fire and get us all there that way?"

"Because, Love, only an Eight-tails can transport other people with them. If I tried, there is a good chance that I could kill you!"

"Oh, right then . . . onwards!" Daima chuckled and followed her as she followed Reytha. He couldn't really complain about his lot in life, in the end. With a friend like Reytha and an ally in Brenna, he couldn't really ask for much more.

****3****

The Forest, which had seemed to stretch on into forever, was in all actuality not very big from where they were to where they wanted to be. In fact, it only stretched out for about ten miles from the dozen mountains at its epicenter. The Mountains were not entirely natural, truth be told. Two rose majestically from the center, with ten smaller ones ringing them. They were each representative of the twelve Great Clans, and the largest two at the epicenter were the homes of the Heads of the Wyrm and Dragon clans, the two most powerful (and Arch-Rivals as well). The other ten housed the Heads of the Clan of Eagle, Phoenix, Stag, Boar, Wolf, Fox, Griffin, Leopard, Bear, and Horse.

And, of course, the Calling of the Forces, which was basically a Council of War, just *had* to take place in the middle of Dragon and Wyrm Mount. Reytha led them both through the rapidly dwindling forest at a fast pace, which would only get more sedate as they started to climb the looming mountain that was in front of them. Brenna used her unstrung bow rather like a walking stick, as both of her companions had gone to being a Fox and wolf.

Smug little bastards.

She stopped abruptly, calling out to her two companions. "Wait . . . wait a moment, alright? I need to . . . to catch my breath . . . a little!"

Nainya gave her a look before reverting back to being Daima, becoming transparent for a second. When he became solid again, he smirked at her, as did Reytha (although her transformation was a little flashier than that of any Naish).

"What's wrong, 'pup'? Lose your breath back there?" Brenna glared at Daima as he mocked her good-naturedly.

"Aye, 'kit', need us to carry you?"

Brenna transferred her glare to the Kitsune woman (she was getting very good at glaring at people, thanks to those two). "Hah hah, very funny. Well, it's not my fault that *I* can't become a wolf or some bloody fox at will!"

Reytha gave her a mock affronted look. "I am a Kitsune, dear, not a fox."

"FINE, A *KITSUNE*!!! I DON'T CARE!!!!!" They both took a step back as she shouted, and Daima rubbed his ear ruefully.

Reytha went and patted her on the shoulder comfortingly. "Yes, sorry Dear, we were just having a little fun. Me and Daima will walk beside you from now on, okay?" Brenna nodded at her, looking a little ashamed at her outburst. Reytha smiled. "Oh, c'mon, no need to be so glum! Besides, we are almost there!" She pointed at the now looming mountain, and the young woman seemed to brighten up a bit. They all set off, walking at a slower clip than before.

Brenna walked beside Reytha, and Daima brought up the rear. Brenna brought her head close to the Kitsune woman. "Say, Reytha . . . who exactly are the Clan Heads? Are they really Gods?"

The woman laughed lightly. "Well . . . not by *human* definition, but, I'm not exactly human, am I? Well, they can be killed, but it's damned hard, by anyone's standards. They each are gigantic animals, at least twenty times as large as their species. Also, they are far more powerful, both in magic and strength. But, a word of advice: tread lightly around them. Any of them can be your worst nightmare if angered, and a good half of them can and will anger easily. You see, there is a rift between us all. It all started back in the mists of time, no one but the clan Heads can remember that far back. I think that the War started between the Wyrm's and Dragon's, and we all took sides. In the end, it was basically between those of us who can use magic, and those who can't. The Wolves and Griffin's were, however, an exception. Wolves, who can not use any magic normally, sided with the foxes, as we were, and still are, ancient allies. And the Griffin's, who hold the power of a Windstorm in their wings, sided with the Horses, most likely because of the Hippogriff's." She stepped carefully over an outlying log, making sure she didn't trip over it, before continuing with her speech. "The Naish, like Daima over there, were founded to keep the peace. You know, a Human bonded to an animal, well then they can be the ones to keep the peace betwixt us all. Of course, Mab threw it all to hell when she attacked with her magic's and enslaved monsters . . . but that's for a brighter day." Indeed, the sun was already drawing closer to the mountains, and the shadows were getting longer.

Daima caught up to the two of them easily. "Pretty soon we'll be making camp. Keep an eye out for a good place; we'll stop as soon as we find one. No use going on in the dark if Brenna can't see it."

Said girl hung her head, feeling like she was holding back the two of her new friends. Reytha wrapped a tail around her shoulders comfortingly, casting a sidelong glare at Daima, who merely looked at her confusedly. Brenna looked up and smiled at her.

After another quarter hour of hiking through the rapidly diminishing forest, they reached a small clearing, large enough to be easy to move in, but small enough to be hard to spot from the outside, as they were shielded by a screen of trees, although a mite too sparse for the liking's of the two shape-shifters. The Forest was a dangerous place to be a human in, and most likely would always be ever since Yamaine had come to power. Killing an ally on accident is still killing them.

Brenna took out her sleeping roll, and laid it on the ground next to Reytha, who was already in her Fox form. Getting into it, she quickly fell asleep next to her friend, who put several of her tails over her protectively.

'*She's not your kit, you know,*' growled Nainya in the language of wolves and foxes.

The Kitsune sighed. Although she liked Daima . . . a lot, she could barely stand Nainya, who was, in a word, blunt. Well, most wolves were, and especially Alpha's, but it didn't mean that she should like it at all, and she didn't. '*No, she isn't. But that doesn't mean that I can't or shouldn't protect her. In here, she is a kit. This is all so new to her, and it will take a while for her to readjust. Until then, I will give her my protection. And, what's wrong with her being my kit?*' The last question was filled with suspicion on the seven-tails part.

Nainya gave her a look. '*Nothing, except for the fact that she is a human.*'

'*Half-human,*' corrected Reytha quickly. '*She is a half-Elf, mind you. And the offspring of Dragon tamers, not your regular heritage. She is strong.*'

'*Either way,*' rumbled the wolf, '*she is not of your clan, and is not going to see you as a mother anytime soon.*'

'*As to the first, there is such a thing as adoption. And, as to the second, I don't really care. I have time in spades . . . after all; I already have almost a millennia behind me . . . what could a few more years hurt?*'

Nainya winced and said, '*I guess your right. But . . . think on it carefully. I do not wish to see you go through heart ache again . . . not like before.*'

'If you are talking about Ganich, I have gotten over it completely. Unlike some, I do not dwell on the past!' She gave a low growl of warning to him, showing Nainya that this was a path that he should tread carefully. Her dead mate was always a touchy subject for her.

'No, I am not speaking of your mate . . . it's just . . . ah, never mind! We can speak on it on the morrow . . . get some sleep, Reytha. I'll take first watch.'

She merely snorted, putting her head on her paws, closing her eyes as sleep overcame her.

Nainya mimicked her, although his yellow eyes remained open and watchful, although that was merely a formality. His nose was better than any sentry, and he knew most scents right off. He rested his great head against his paws, and began his watch. He cast his gaze one last time over the two sleeping females.

'Sleep well, old friend. Sleep well.'

Maybe things would turn out all right . . . in the end.

****4****

Brenna snuggled deeper into the warm something's that surrounded her. They felt like blankets, very, very warm blankets. Just then she realized that she was supposed to be in the middle of the forest, where there were no blankets. Or, at least, none that she had. Her eyes snapped open to the sight of seven large tails wrapped around her, as if they were her guardians against the world. She tried to move her arms, and found them to be held tightly against her sides. She struggled against her bindings, but to no avail.

Finally, she let out a small grunt as her efforts began to take a toll. Immediately the tails were off set, and went off of her. She turned around to see Reytha, in her true Kitsune form. A flash, and there again stood the woman that Brenna had come to know as a friend, even in such a short time. "Are you alright, *Huiliyn*?"

Brenna cocked her head to one side, but then shook it off. A strange word, most likely Elvish. No matter, though. "Um . . . no, I was just startled is all."

Reytha gave a genuine smile at her. "That's good. I thought that you could use the warmth . . . it gets cold out here, sometimes, y'know." If it was an attempt at an energetic comment, then it had fallen flat on its proverbial face.

"Um . . . sure . . . where's Daima?" She asked out of part desperation to change the subject, and part curiosity. The shape-shifter was no where to be seen.

Both women were uncomfortable now over the entire situation. "He's . . . getting firewood, I think."

"Oh . . . good. Need a fire, out here."

"Yeah," agreed Reytha. She then muttered something about needing to get some meat, and took off.

Brenna stared after her. *'What a strange person.'*

*   *   *

Daima grunted as he strained with the heavy pile of deadwood. It was piled high in his arms, a great stack of things that would burn and dance merrily for their entertainment. To an outsider, he seemed to be at ease, if a little sweaty due to his burden.

But Nainya was not on his outside. He was not only Daima's best friend (you kind of have to be, what-with the whole being inside of him thing), but knew when he was troubled, which just happened to be at that moment. *"Daima? What is wrong?"*

Instead of outwardly speaking, Daima thought his answers back to his brother (which comes in a bit handy when you need to converse without anyone knowing). *'Nothing at all. Why do you ask?'*

Nainya sighed as best he could. *"Don't give me that. Something is wrong. If anything, I can smell it easily, even without the odd, oh, twenty or so years that we have been bonded together. What's wrong? Honestly."*

Daima shook his head. *'You can be very annoying at times, you know that?'*

"And do you know that you are avoiding the question?"

He smiled, showing his somewhat elongated canine teeth. *'Yeah. Well . . . something doesn't seem right about this.'*

"What, Brenna? Or Reytha?"

'No, not them. Just . . . I don't know, this whole big mess of things that we're in.'

"If you haven't noticed, if we weren't in this whole big mess we'd most like be dead? I can't count the times when someone on our side has saved our respective asses."

'I know . . . and that's just it. I get the feeling that . . . I don't know, that we did something wrong. I . . . had a nightmare, when I receded.'

The wolf snickered lightly. *"Awww, poor pup . . . want me to fight away the monsters?"*

Daima started walking back towards camp, still arguing jokingly with his other half. *'Shut up, lithuine! Since when did you become my conscience?'*

"Since we first bonded! And you have no right to call me an idiot, it's like insulting yourself!"

Daima sighed outwardly, breaking the relative silence of the woods. *'Okay . . . first, lithuine means jackass, so get your Elvish right. Second . . . I saw Glendiuen.'*

All showings of humor left the wolf as he realized the consequences of this. *"Are you saying that you suddenly have the Sight?"*

'No, no! Just . . . I shouldn't be relieving such painful memories in the Dreamscape? Isn't it a place to . . . well, relax and keep your sanity from the toils of living with you?'

"I resent that," responded Nainya, eliciting a small chuckle from Daima. "I will inform you that I am a very agreeable person to live with! Seriously though . . . I don't remember all that much of Glendiuen, as you did most of the fighting there. But . . . what part do you remember the most?"

'Just before . . . when Rothgar was taken. I could never forget that.'

". . . Show me."

'Alright . . . first, let's get back to camp.' Nainya remained silent, indicating his approval. And his apprehension.

If Daima had the Sight . . . things could get very, very dangerous for the both of them. Seers rarely lived past thirty.

It watched them from afar. Its scent was dampened by the Will of its master. She called it . . . she ordered it.

Let the blood flow.

Its eyes were lifeless . . . and, its soul was trapped inside of its own body. It was a vessel for the will of its master. Nothing else mattered, now. It had its orders, and it would fulfill them. It had to. It was a puppet . . . a second-born golem. Its life before possession was just a happy memory. It did nothing that its master did not order, and it did nothing that She forbid. It wouldn't. It couldn't.

Learn this lesson well, my pet . . . that urchin before thee is a nuisance to me . . . remove it, and all of its little half-breed friends.

As you will it, Mistress.

It moved with a stealth and swiftness that bellied its huge bulk and strength. It hungered for blood. It lusted for blood. So, blood it would spill.

Let the blood flow, let all the Enemies burn in the fires of their 'Perfection', their shattered sense of self. Because this one held no illusions.

Brenna smiled as he returned, carrying a rather large pile of wood in his arms. "Ah, Daima, how—"

"Where's Reytha?"

Brenna's brow creased in a frown that never showed in her face, because her slight smile never faltered, but her eyes showed it true. "Well, she went off to—"

"Here I am!" Reytha carried three rabbits by the scruffs of their necks, swinging them merrily as if she were bringing presents to all of the little children. "What's up?" Her huge grin faltered at seeing Daima's huge frown, and disappeared entirely at what he said next.

"I need to Descend. Now."

Reytha gasped. "Are you sure? It is very dangerous to do it outside of a city. We may not be able to get you back if your strength falters."

"I know, but this is important. Please. We need to speak, face to face."

"Wait," said Brenna confusedly. "What is this . . . Descending? It sounds difficult . . . and time consuming."

"Yes it is, and we'll manage. Explaining it will take more time than doing it, so you'll have to wait until we are climbing the mountain. Now, this will take a minute, so watch carefully. It is the old ways . . . the Blood Magic. Lucky for you," said Reytha, turning back towards Daima, "I am a Kitsune."

"For which I am ever thankful, and now can we do this?" He was getting impatient, which was odd for him.

"Alright." No witticism, no sarcastic comments. Reytha was serious, which, again, was an oddity.

Brenna could sum it up in three words: They were screwed.

Reytha bit her thumb with one of her sharp canines, letting a little blood flow onto it. Then, she spread the blood around Daima's neck, watching as it flowed down, covering his neck in a sheath of crimson. He sat cross-legged on the ground, and she walked around him, placing five drops of blood around him, equally distanced. When she was finished with that, she placed a dot on his forehead, yet it did not flow, so potent was the blood magic. Reytha got down on her knees and clenched her hands together, as if praying. Daima closed her eyes as she began her chanting, in an ethereal, sing-song voice.

"*Heret, knowlden, angelis, ku. Heret, yulach, jalom, niden, ku.*" Lines of white fire, pure as first fallen snow, spread out under Daima, interlocking, flowing, forming a pentagram under and around him. Suddenly, the light engulfed him! Brenna forced herself not to scream, not knowing what damage could happen then if she did. When the light ended, Daima slumped down, the lines receded into the shadow of the dawn, and Reytha bowed down gratefully, panting heavily.

At Brenna's questioning look, Reytha said, "It is done. It's all up to him, now."

"Okay. What now?"

"Well, we—" She stopped as there was a low rustling from the sparse leaves, and a low, animalistic growl. "RUN!!!! I'll handle this!" Then, the ogre burst out of the trees.

He stumbled a little as he landed; Descending always took a lot out of him, both physically and mentally. A shape came out of the mist that blanketed the land, and he went up to it. The Shadow resolved itself into the shape of a large wolf. A large black wolf, with piercing yellow eyes.

He went up and scratched Nainya behind the ears, eliciting a growl of pleasure from the great Alpha. "Remind me why I am *always* the one who gets thrown down here, while you set it up?"

Although his mouth didn't move a bit, Daima heard his bond-brother as clear as day. *"Maybe because I cannot sit like you can? Or maybe it's the fur. Actually, it's always the fur."*

Daima chuckled at him. Nainya tried to act noble and wise, but around his friends, he showed himself to be nothing more than an over-grown wolf pup. "Yes, it's probably because everyone finds you so cute and fluffy." Nainya merely growled, and Daima scratched behind his ear even more.

"I am neither *cute nor fluffy. I am a noble descendant of hunters and warriors!"*

"Why can't warriors be cute or fluffy?" Daima chuckled as Nainya shook his great head in annoyance.

"You damn child. But, we're getting off track. Follow me." He set off into the mist, setting an easy pace that still set Daima jogging after his bond-brother. After a few minutes of this, they came to a great stone basin. Using the ledge to help him up, Nainya used his nose to point at the cloudy water within it. *"Show me."*

". . . Alright. But you may not like it." Summoning up a little magic, Daima placed a hand on the still surface. It resolved itself into an image, and the two viewed this:

The smell of smoke and fire was pungent and sharp to his nose, just as the cries of the dying cut through the air and assaulted his ears. He wore no helmet, as it had been ripped off after the first few minutes of battle, being more hindrance than help to one of his abilities. His sword was held up, alert and wary of any steeled death sent towards him. It was by now red and bloodied, but not dented at all; its craftsmanship was too good. That elf had done his job well.

Daima ducked under an arrow, looking around for anywhere he could make himself of good use to anyone on his side. Humans of the King's army, along with Elves, Dwarves, and a few animals of the Wold fought valiantly against Mab's army, a ragged assortment of ogres, giants, goblins, and other such nasty beasts from beyond the border. He cut the legs out from a rather tall goblin, right before an Elf bashed its head in with her swords blunt edge. One would do well not to piss off an Elf. She smiled her thanks before turning back to the battle. An arrow sailed into her eye, and she fell to the ground, writhing in pain. Contorting his fingers for a moment, he muttered the words that started the spell of Release. Recognition was evident in her remaining eye, and she weakly nodded her head, hair now dirty with mud, gore and blood. "Kai." The Elf lurched up for a moment, and then passed on. No one could have helped her then; the arrow had gone too far in to be removed.

Those damned archers were cutting them deeply. They really weren't good marksman, having trouble hitting the broad side of a wall from twenty paces, but there were just too damned many of them. A few hundred yards away, a giant was laying about indiscriminately into the poor bastards that were scurrying about its feet with a ten foot club. Arrows were piercing its hide, enough to make it appear as a pincushion, but they didn't seem to bother it all that much. It roared in anger as a spear went deeply into its side, one of the few places where its thick hide didn't give it nigh on impenetrable protection.

Daima smiled grimly, and went onwards. His lips curled upwards in a feral snarl, a reminder of his other half. 'Soon, Nainya. Soon.' He wove his way in and out of the battle ground inside of Glendiuen, wetting his sword bloody a few more times. Another arrow flew right past his ear, but he ignored it. He'd gotten used to it by now. A rather ugly troll challenged him, growling out its disapproval at his existence. Its small eyes were even duller than a normal trolls, if possible, showing Mab's power over it true. All it knew now were fighting and dying. To prove this point, it swung a rather large axe at his vulnerable skull. No helmet could have stopped that blow, and even if it could, his neck would still snap like a twig. He dodged right, rolling tightly. His sword flashed down and rent the creatures leg, leaving a long scar in the flesh, sore and bleeding. With a roar of pain and hatred, the troll swung at waist level, perhaps trying to catch him off-guard. It didn't, as he was already out of its range.

Abruptly, it fell with a grunt onto its back, with an axe sticking out from the back of its knee. A dwarf, only half of Daima's height, pulled it out. In a show of bravery or stupidity (or both), he stood on its chest, and raised his axe high above his head. It crashed down right 'twixt the troll's eyes with a sickening thud, and black blood splattered everywhere. When the dwarf turned, Daima saw him to be Rothgar, the Dwarven King's axe-bearer. His eyes were red from weeping.

With a sinking feeling in the pit of his stomach, Daima went up to him. "So . . . is Jhilh . . ."

A loud sniff interrupted him. It was a rare sight to see a stoic dwarf warrior crying, and one that he hoped to never to see again. "Aye, he was felled by nigh on a score of goblin's . . . the bastards surrounded *him before I could protect him. I have . . . failed! Now, I must seek death, so as to rejoin my master. Fare thee well, Naish, I will not see the next dawning!"* An axe—bearer was assigned to a Dwarven Prince at birth, and was sworn to be his companion and bodyguard until death. If one failed, they were consumed with suck grief that they would seek death in order to be at peace with this great burden. Rothgar had lost more than his best friend, he had lost his will to live.

There was nothing he could do. Turning, Daima raced back to the battle.

He fought with a renewed vigor, having seen two of his friends die just then, or as good as. He stabbed an ogre in the gut; the great beast already marked and scared by numerous cuts from others blades. In one hand a club was held loosely, already carrying a few extra spear and arrow heads in it. This was, truly, a monster. But, not because of the blood it had spilled, no, that was not what set it apart. It was its eyes. They were dull, lifeless . . . as one already dead.

He had no problem at all helping it along. No, none at all.

Then, the shadow came upon him. He screamed. A shape . . . a shadow . . . and a shriek to jar the dead in their hollows. He closed his eyes, and waited for Death to come and claim him . . .

As the image faded into the grey nothingness of before, they looked at each other, the enormity of this situation dawning on them. *"So . . . it is possible that you may have the sight. Relive your memories . . . and when those are done, you relive memories of the future . . ."*

Despite it all, Daima chuckled. "You realize that that made absolutely no sense at all?"

"You know what I mean!" The wolf went on to mumble something about insolence. Suddenly, he sniffed. *"Something is wrong. I smell . . . fear, from those two. And . . . the Shadow. You must away!"*

"Alright, I'll be gone in a second." As he settled himself, gathering up the energy to return, Nainya called out to him.

"Remember! The Old Magic, the Blood Magic, flows strongest within us!" Daima nodded to his friend as he faded away.

Reytha was having a hard time of it. She had already reverted to her seven-tails form, as a fox had an easier time dodging the monster club that the ogre used. Her tails were sharp as spears, but they didn't seem to bother it. It merely looked on her with its dull eyes as it sought to crush her beneath its weapon. She tried to concentrate enough to make her magic's, but that pesky club, which now resembled a overly-large tree limb, kept trying to get her. Bastard.

She jumped back, yet again, from its swing, and the club buried itself in the soft ground, but it was out yet again just as quickly. She growled at it to try to get a rise from it, but it shrugged off the challenge. *I can't keep this up forever!* Her tails pierced the hide over its stomach again, but it didn't even flinch. Unfortunately, she had kept them in a mite too long.

It grabbed two of her tails, pulling them out roughly and holding her at arms length. A slow smile spread over its dull face as it readied that damned club again. Well, at least she could concentrate now.

Fortunately for her, something *did* break her concentration, but not the expected skull crushing blow. It was a green-fletched arrow, one of Brenna's, and it sailed into the beast's eye, and it gave off a roar of pain. It dropped Reytha and frantically grabbed at the offending object, seeking to pull it out at any cost. Another arrow came at it, but that damned club managed to block it. Reytha took a moment to gather her wits.

As Brenna launched another arrow, she smirked at Reytha. The Kitsune did not bother to dignify that with a response, but instead continued to prepare for her spell. A nice little affair that would make its innards burst into flame.

Unfortunately for the both of them, the ogre managed to pull the arrow—severed eye and all—from its socket. With a renewed bellow of rage, it charged at them. A flash, a cry of pain, and a sound of a sword un-sheathing, and it stumbled a few more steps before falling flat on its face, its innards spilling out on the ground, bathed in the dust and dawn. When it was over, a shadow slinked out, burning up in the sun. Daima looked both of them in the eyes before wiping his sword on the leaves, getting rid of most of the blood that was on it. He turned to Reytha, sheathing his blade. "This . . . is not good."

"Do you even need to say it?" She was, by now, in her human form, all seven tails almost dragging on the ground as the battle rush wore off.

"Wait . . . why is this bad?"

"Well—" He was cut off as a sharp report of thunder, closely following a lightning strike, and both of them looked graver still. "We'll explain on the way! We have to get gone from here, NOW!!!" He started off at a jog, letting the other two catch up before increasing his pace. Before long, they all three were sprinting.

****5****

They were beaten down savagely by the wind, which was howling through the rocks of the mountain. They were strung out in a line, Daima at the front, Reytha at the end, and Brenna in the middle. Her bow was slung over her shoulder, and her green-feathered arrows were hidden by a sheath, of sorts to keep them from flying away. It was a leather flap, tied by a string to the bottom, and it had the dual effect of keeping them dry and within easy reach. They all three of them had their heads bowed to the howling gale.

"Where are we?" Although she shouted, her voice was carried away by the wind. Nonetheless, Reytha heard it (she does have the hearing of a fox, after all).

"Somewhere on Boar, I think!" Brenna could barely hear it over the pounding wind, but managed to catch it. She nodded to show that she understood.

Stopping short, Daima pointed at a little alcove a few dozen yards ahead on the path. No words were spoken 'twixt them, but none was needed. It was easy enough to understand. They bowed their heads again, and made their way towards the small bit of salvation. Hopefully, that is.

As it turned out, that small "alcove" was actually a twelve foot deep cave. The rain, which was driving down at a hard angle to the side, barely penetrated a few feet. They squished into the back, and Reytha used some magic to light a fire. They had found some deadwood at the back, and kept that in reserve from what they had stored in their packs. "Oh, yay!" Reytha sounded like a happy little child as she pulled out three rabbits that didn't look too drenched.

Daima snorted. "You kept those things?"

She huffed in good natured annoyance and put her hands on her hips. "I'll have you know that I haven't had a good rabbit in months!"

"Yeah, they're not good 'cause you can't cook for a damn!'"

"Better than you can!"

"I have a bloody wolf inside me! I can afford to eat meat raw!"

"No you can't! Only Nainya can!"

"And he is a part of me!"

"Uh . . . guys?" She flinched as they both yelled at her, but gave a small giggle. "If you want . . . I can cook. Everyone at the inn said I was pretty good."

After giving her a look, Reytha said, "Alright, lets see what ya got!" Brenna looked sadly at their meager provisions: Three rabbits, two loaves of bread, and a few apples. And all she had was a cooking pot and a wooden spoon. Joy.

After an hour of cooking, she announced ready, knocking Daima out of his nap. Reytha had been meditating . . . or something of that sort, Brenna honestly had no idea. She doled out the soupy mix onto the bread pieces, and each held at least a dozen rabbit pieces on it. Reytha took a moment to sniff it before taking a bite out of her bread, swallowing it with gusto. After she finished it, she licked her lips. "That's good. Nice job, Brenna!" She then started on her other two pieces.

Daima chuckled a bit at his friend. "Hungry, Reytha?" He was silenced by a rumble from his own stomach, and the Kitsune woman smirked at him.

"Look who's talking, Mister I Can Take Anything For Any Amount of Time!" Daima gave her a glare before taking a bite. His eyes lit up in surprise, and then he wolfed down the rest. "S'ch gud!" Brenna took a moment to decipher it before smiling at him. Then, she took to her three pieces. Who knew when their next true meal would be?

Later on, Reytha and Brenna both stared at the waning storm. It was letting up . . . a little bit, at any rate. Behind them, Daima was laying against the far wall, wrapped up in a warm fur blanket that Brenna had carried with her. They two had their backs to the fire, but spared a glance to him from time to time. There was a silence between the two, both to wrapped up in their own thoughts to speak much on anything.

After another few minutes, Brenna spoke. "I guess that that spell that he did took more out of him then he thought."

A quiet laugh, and Reytha answered. "Oh, no. He knew how much he was weakened; he was just bull-shiting his way through, mostly."

"Why?"

Another laugh, this one deeper. "Because he's a man, of course! He has an image to keep up!" She snorted, eliciting a small smile from

Brenna. "Bloody fool." Another pause, as Brenna bit her lip, looking deep in thought. "Something on your mind?"

Brenna smiled a little, but once again frowned. "Reytha . . . I don't mean to pry, but . . . what exactly are you and Daima? I can't figure it out."

Reytha sighed, and laid back, hands on her stomach. "Well . . . it's a bit . . . complicated, I guess. You see, we are friends from a decade or so ago. We have saved the others life so many times that I've lost count. He and Nainya . . . well, I guess I look on him like a brother, of sorts, and the same with Nainya, although maybe a bit less so. He is . . . well, he is a bit of a mystery to me, although I have lived far longer than him. And, that's the problem with befriending mortals. They will all, eventually, pass on. And I've already died, so I guess that I can't pass on like that again."

"What do you mean . . . that you've already died?" Brenna stopped herself from backing away as she eyed the Kitsune.

Said fox spirit laughed at her. "Heh, well I guess that takes a bit of explanation, doesn't it? Well, here's how it is, in a nutshell: When a Fox dies; their spirit doesn't go to the Spirit Plane, unlike most peoples. Instead, it is . . . reincarnated; I guess you could say, in another body, except they can now use magic and have two tails. Tails are gained under special circumstances. The first five are all the same for every which one of us. The first is the Tail of Birth, next comes the Tail of Death. Then . . . Tail of Blood-Letting, for your first enemy killed in battle. Then . . . Tail of Mercy, for sparing an enemy. The Fifth . . . is the Tail of Healing, for bringing back a body from Death's Door. The last four Tails are specific to each one of us. You have to perform great deeds, acts of love, bravery, courage, and the like."

"Aren't bravery and courage the same?" The girl looked terribly confused, but it was a lot to take in all at once.

"No. Not in the slightest, although they both can deal with battle. Bravery is the willingness to kill someone, for love or for loyalty. And courage . . . is the willingness to die for those same reasons. Courage is the most highly regarded in some circles, but bravery in most others." Reytha sighed again and sat up, leaning on her left arm for support. "I guess this all a mite confusing, eh?"

She reluctantly nodded her head. "Yeah . . . a little."

Reytha affectionately ruffled her long hair. "Yeah, but you'll get used to it."

Before they could speak more on such matters more, an ear-splitting shriek rent the calming air irreparably, and it sounded as if someone's soul was being torn from their body. Slowly. It was a cry of loss, of hate . . . of pain. It was the cry of a Dragon dying.

"C'mon!" Before she could be stopped, Brenna had rushed out, bow in hand and a green-fletched arrow already nocked to her string. Reytha, after one more forlorn glance at the still sleeping Daima, she took off after her friend.

He stumbled, if possible, on the wing, trying to find a good place to land. To fight, or hide, or both in due course. He chanced a look back at the two Wyrm's which followed him closely, trying to land him and tear into him with their cruel claws . . .

It was too close, and too soon, to use his fire. He had used it taking out the third member, and now he had to catch his breath a bit. And, even if he could, they were too close to do it safely. His wing was torn a little, yet it still worked fine, and there was a long mark of soon to scar flesh, showing underneath his bright blue scales. The armor that had fared him so well in his younger years was now slowly shoring off, now that he had reached maturity. But; it was an unfair exchange: for slightly toughened armor, he had to wait up to two months almost completely un-armored. It was as if the bastards had planned it all along . . .

No time to reminisce now, nor ever more if he didn't put on a turn of speed. The Wyrm's were built heavier, and were slightly slower than he. But, on the flip side, they had a greater endurance for hard flying. They were, slowly, gaining on him. Behind him, he could hear their foul tongues calling to him, giving challenges that normally he would have accepted readily. But, not this night. **"Come, come out, Fair-wing,"** they mocked, insulting his scales, his sires. They were a shade of green so dull and ugly that it bordered on gray. Probably why they had gotten the jump on him. **"What, now? Art thou scared of us? We promise not to hurt thee, oh Lord of Flight and Fire. Come here, or we shall get thee gone from this mountain!"**

He turned his head to them, getting slightly more alarmed at their renewed proximity to his tail, which hung gracefully behind him. **"And I say, get thou gone, Louts! Flee, and fie upon thee! I know no fear but Fafnir, my Liege. Come again when I am full formed, thee foul-winged cowards!"** If he was going down, then he would make sure that they knew what they were: Egg-crushers and The Predators of the Weak. The strength of the Dragon clan will not be tarnished! He cast a now idle eye down upon the far off ground, and realized that it wasn't so far off anymore. They were over a mountain . . . one of the twelve.

Too late, anyway.

He rolled off to the side, screeching out a cry of challenge, and charging the two abruptly. Not expecting any such attack so soon, they tried to mimic him, but to no avail. His iron-strong claws ripped cruelly into their sides, sending blood upon the rain-washed ground. But, Wyrms are strong, and not overly burdened by pain . . . or an overly large brain, for that matter. But fighting was what they knew, and knew it well they did, as if they were bred for it. Most likely, they were. They came up at him from two sides, and he decided on a simple strategy: Divide and Conquer. He decided to take on the slightly larger one first, so that he may show his bravery and courage true.

The Honor of he, nor the Clan of Dragons, would not be tarnished this day!!!

He charged that one, but it was ready, diving out of his way, damn it to Hell. They charged again, and their claws met in midair, claws clashing and teeth gnashing against each other. The Wyrm's breath stank of rot and the foul flesh of its prey. They sprang back, and the Dragon ducked under the smaller ones attack, which was more like a suicide charge. His claws raked across its side, and more blood was spilled onto the mountain side. The Wyrm screeched in pain, and the larger one rounded on the attack again. He danced around this attack, as well, biting the Wyrm's wing with his sharp teeth.

Then it all went to Hell. The smaller one snuck up on him, letting the larger and stronger attack him as a distraction. It latched itself in his blind spot, biting down cruelly on his neck, drawing his sweet, warm, red blood, its sharp claws gouging his sides. All seemed lost . . . so he decided to do all he could.

If he was to die this day, then he would make sure that at least one would die with him. He folded his wings as best he could, rolling so that his back—with the conveniently placed Wyrm on it—faced the hard, uninviting, and rapidly encroaching ground. It did not have time to gather its wits enough to even scream, let alone fly away. So, when they hit the ground with a sickening thud, the Dragon took a quiet satisfaction knowing that the Wyrm had gotten the worst of it. Little bastard deserved it.

Enraged, the last—and largest of the lot of them—Wyrm charged wildly down at him, intent on avenging his comrade who had met such an ignonimus death at the claws of this Dragon. That is, it would have, if an arrow hadn't pierced its eye right then. Still having some wherewithal, the Dragon breathed deep, ignoring the pain in his chest, and blew a stream of flames at his foe. They engulfed the Wyrm, and it unleashed a hideous shriek, and a slightly more hideous stench. After a moment longer airborne, it crashed to earth in an explosion of flesh and fire. Two creatures ran up to him, a kitsune and a girl, who had apparently unleashed the arrow. But that didn't matter that much: he was too tired to care. They yelled something to him, but he didn't have the will to answer. Sleep overcame him, and then engulfed him, unconsciousness releasing the pain to memory . . . for now. Or forever. It all depended whether or not he died.

Reytha sighed as she helped Brenna push the Dragon off of the Wyrm's carcass. She grimaced when she saw the gore that clung to him, a bit of it his own. She turned to her foolhardy comrade. "We won't be able to move him much; he's too heavy for any of us, even all three together. We don't have much choice, unless we leave him here."

"How could you even think of leaving him?!?!?!" Brenna was absolutely flippant at the prospect.

"I didn't say we would. Listen . . . go get Daima, and bring him here, alright? We could use the help. I'll see how bad this is for our newest friend. Go on, shoo!" She flicked her on the head good-naturedly, then turned to her work, frowning slightly. Brenna took off down the path. The wind had died down some, but it was still a mite uncomfortable. Either Brenna was a great shot (possible), or that was some of the best dumb luck that the Kitsune had ever seen (probably). She sighed again. "Now, what shall I do with you?" The Dragon remained stoically unconscious before her. "Thought so."

This was going to be a long, long day. And the Gathering was only two days off.

Daima rolled over, still asleep, as something jabbed his ribs. His hand went up sloppily, trying to grasp the offending object. It responded by jabbing him again, harder. "Wake up!" He muttered something groggily; hand still groping about for whatever the Hell it was that was poking him, which it had done yet again. That something was Brenna's bow, the end of which she was using to jab, repeatedly, the sleeping Naish, hard in the ribs. Finally, after the seventh poke at him, she got pissed off and simply kicked him in the gut. *That* got him to wake up!

Hell hath no fury like a woman who is angry. He was doubled over on the ground, clutching his stomach and gasping for breath. Just when she was about to kick him again (this time in the head), he looked up at her and asked, "What was that for?"

"It doesn't matter, now come ON! We need your help!"

He yawned. "What for?" He remained resolutely on the ground, which only caused her to whack him over the head with her bow. "OUCH!"

"There is an unconscious and probably dying Dragon outside, and we need your help healing him! Get up or I shall kick you again!" For added emphasis, she moved her foot back into position.

Pushing his hands out pleadingly, he quickly got up and out, muttering something about crazy girls. *"Heh, seems like she owns you now!"*

'Shut up, you flea covered urchin!'

"Temper, temper!" Nainya chuckled maddeningly inside of his head. *"Mustn't be too angry, or Brenna will get you!"*

'I SAID SHUT UP!!!!!' Nainya took the hint, but not before snickering one last time at his friends expense. Brenna tugged impatiently on his arm, leading him to the scene.

When he saw the blue tinged creature, covered in what he assumed was its own blood, he paled. There was going to be Hell to pay for this. He immediately went up to Reytha, who was trying her hands (and tails) at removing a rather large bone spike from the Dragon. After a couple of minutes of pushing and pulling, the two had gotten it out, casting it aside as Reytha set about healing it with her considerable magic's.

They went about that for a few more minutes, all three of them removing the bones from the exploded Wyrm. It wasn't much of a problem until the Dragon woke up.

It abruptly reared its noble head, still dripping with the gore of its enemies. Shakily getting up on four legs, he reared up on his two hind legs, revealing his underside to be of a duller blue than his top, so as to blend into the sky. He was roaring out a challenge, screaming his defiance, once again, unto the heavens. And they, once again, deemed not to answer. He then cast his eye on the three beings that stood on one side of him. Two of them tried not to show their fear, but he could smell it, like the stench of sweat and blood. But the last, and quite obviously the youngest of them—and, *Human* no less!—held no fear of him at all. Indeed, she approached him with border lining awe upon her face. Obviously, she had no clue what she was dealing with. He took a moment to smell the air, and found the storm to have moved on, probably going to make sport of some weary travelers somewhere.

He turned his face to her, neck straining slightly. **"Who art thou, Human, to come to this place?"**

She took a moment to look taken aback at his ability to speak, not quite sure how words could form intelligibly behind all of those teeth, but then bowed humbly to him. "Forgive our intrusion, Lord Dragon. We saw your plight with those . . . um, Wyrms . . . and decided to help. Just now, we were tending to your wounds, which were considerable. My name . . . is Brenna'Adun'Kial."

"Why doth thou speak such lies? Any can see that thou art but a human!" Smoke began to curl around his snout, giving him an, if possible, even more alarming visage.

She still held no fear, which was downright infuriating. "Oh, but it is true! I am a half-elf!"

Taking that as their cue, her two friends rushed up. Reytha, tails in clear view behind her, bowed low to him. One does not confront a dragon lightly. "It *is* the truth! She was only found not three days ago in a Human inn, being raised at them with no regard to her true self."

He took a moment to sniff the Kitsune, and was satisfied that there was no lie in her speech. **"As may be true. But . . . why is she here? Should she not first meet with her kin?"** Reytha leaned in and whispered something to him, and his head momentarily bowed in sadness and regret. He turned to the girl, who stood behind Daima now, although not of her own will. The great head bowed, sinuous and graceful. **"My apologies, friend; I was mistook. If I may, would you mind continuing? It appears that my wounds are indeed grave."**

Brenna took a moment to figure out what he had said, before bowing again. "Of course . . . ?"

"Dedira is my name, Brenna'Adun'Kial."

"Just Brenna, please, Dedira." She smiled sweetly at him, and she and her friends went back to work, plying their skills at another large piece of bone fragment that stuck out of Dedira's back, near the tail. He tried to take the pain with a stoic silence, but couldn't hold it all in. He roared out again, but this time in agony. Brenna immediately rushed to his head and stroked him on the eye bone, calming him a bit. Turning back to Reytha, who had stopped along with Daima. "Isn't there anything that you can give him to stop the pain? Surely there is something!"

Reytha sighed and wiped her brow, which was beaded with sweat. "Nothing at the moment. And, besides, stopping the pain would most likely stop his heart as well. I can heal wounds of the body, but pain is a part of life. Stop the pain, and I stop his heart. I am sorry, Lord Dedira, but you will simply have to take the pain as it is. Brenna, comfort him, would you? You *do* have Dragon Tamers blood in you, after all."

Brenna nodded, and started stroking Dedira's eye bone again, whispering soothing words at him as the Daima and Reytha began pulling out the bone fragment again. Dedira winced as it grated against his already frayed flesh, but knew he would have to just take it . . . although Brenna helped a lot, just by being there. He could smell it, now, that odd tang that only Dragon Tamer's had about them, and he felt the aura from her lineage. He again wanted to roar, to scream his agony out as the bone fragment slid out of him, but managed to die it down to a whimper that died at his lips.

He winced as they pulled out another shard of bone from his wing, and felt the hole there heal up with new skin and muscle. This went on for almost an hour, but it felt an eternity. The last, and worst, injury to him was a broken left wing, which they managed to set properly, and Reytha speeded the healing a bit so it could only take a week or so. She wiped her hands on her leggings, leaving behind a smear of both blood and gore there. She smiled at him, and patted him good naturedly on the head, smiling all the wider when he growled at her. "Good news, Dedira: We managed to get all of those sharp bones out of, but there is also a bit of bad to that, as well. You see, your left wing was broken in two places. I managed to set it, but it will take a week to heal, at least, so no flying for a bit. Also, take it easy, alright? You've got a lot of new muscle, now, from all the healing, so don't stretch them too far or you will regret it. Any questions?" The Dragon shook his head, and Reytha smiled. "Good." She promptly passed out from magic exhaustion, straight into Daima's arms. He gently set her down, shaking his head and frowning.

"She worked herself almost to death," he stated to no one in particular. "That must be a Hell of a lot of magic there, as seven tails don't exhaust so easily." With a flash of fire, Reytha went back into her fox-form, curled up in a ball with her tails used as both pillows and blankets.

"What do you mean, seven tails'? I count eight, unless thou art prithee to a new system of which I was never told of." Daima looked at the Dragon as if he had suddenly sprouted an extra few heads. Then, he glanced down at Reytha, and, indeed, she had grown in another tail. He chuckled, before picking her up, casting about for a good place to set her down in. Suddenly, Dedira's head hove into his view. **"If I may? Set her upon my back, and I shall carry her to the Gathering. That is where thou art going, correct?"**

Daima smiled thankfully at the Dragon. "Yes it is, thanks. Just let me get our things, and then we'll be off." He set her down near where Dedira's neck met his shoulder's, creating a handy little nook there. Reytha got comfortable there, still sleeping heavily. Daima took off, down the path.

Dedira lumbered down the path, Reytha still sleeping away her exhaustion on his broad back. His wings were folded up at his side, although the left one was folded awkwardly, because of its being broken. Daima and Brenna carried their packs easily on their backs, still lamenting the notorious lack of food. The sun was still high above them, and the end of the valley that they traversed was in sight. It led out of Boar Mount, although they still had to climb halfway up the Dragon's Mount before they could truly rest. Abruptly, Brenna turned to Dedira.

"Excuse me, but, how much longer do we have for walking? I never knew, and Daima hasn't been this way in years, so his memory is a bit fuzzy."

"Ah, 'tis a great place. Between the ten Mountains and the Great Two of Dragon and Wyrm lies a vale, forested and full of game. It is only a mile at its widest, although it fills an area nigh on the space of a quarter of the forest. In other words, large."

Brenna gave him a confused look. "But, then it can't be all that big, then! When we three went through the forest, it couldn't be more than fifteen miles!" The great beast shook with laughter, and she glared pointedly at him. "What? What's so funny?"

Dedira shook his head, as if to rid it of some flies around it. **"My apologies, dear heart. You see, where you three passed was the narrowest point possible. The Forest itself is untouched for hundreds of miles. I could fly day and night for three days and not see the end of it. No, thou art misled, dear-heart. Please, accept my apology, as it was uncouth of me to poke fun at thy ignorance, which had no reason nor whim to be corrected."**

"Oh . . . I accept, Dedira. Thank you."

They all walked on in silence for a few minutes more, the silence a little uncomfortable, but not much. A small cloud of dust rose from behind Dedira, him being much heavier than your average traveler. A spot of vibrant green assailed their eyes, assaulting them with the sheer unadulterated brightness of it all. Then, it passed from view. Daima took that as his cue to leave them. He handed his pack to Brenna, saying, "Well, I'm off to scout," before changing into Nainya, who promptly padded off.

They stared after him a moment, before Brenna commented, "Well, that was rude!"

"Too true, dear-heart. I heartily agree." She smiled at him, looked in on the still unconscious Kitsune, then shrugged on the extra pack. It really didn't make much of a difference, truth to tell.

After a few more minutes walking, they saw the full extent of the Vale. Brenna gaped at it open mouthed, and Dedira sighed happily. He was almost home. **"Welcome, dear heart . . . to Wold."**

6

Brenna gazed around herself in wonder, mouth still conspicuously open at the sight around and before her. Graceful oak trees, their green tops swaying gently in the breeze, competed for sun with the gentle whites of some trees she had never viewed before. There was enough space between them all to allow sunlight to stream down onto the bushes that covered the ground. It was a haven for anything that chose to live there. Elk grazed on the copious amounts of grass that were there, and she heard the scampering of hares in the underbrush, and the howl of wolves in the distance. A fox, a single solitary tail behind it, looked warily at them before running off to hunt the hares that seemed to make a good living there.

But the most glorious thing of the entire affair was the two gigantic mountains, which put the one they had just ascend to shame, rising up not far from where they stood. Brenna took an involuntary step back in awe, bumping into the Dragon's foreleg. He chuckled. **"Impressed, dearling?"**

"Very much so." She shook her head to relieve it of the image of perfection. She had learned long ago that perfection was one of the cruelest illusions of all. "So . . . do we wait for that damned Naish, or go on to the mountain?"

"Why doth thou ask this of me? I am but a youngling by our standards, only forty years of age."

"How. The. HELL! Can you say that? You. Are. Forty. YEARS OLD!!! I am SIXTEEN!!!!" She made sure to ground out each and every word to Dedira, and it was his turn to take a step back. If she had known how hard it was to intimidate a Dragon, Brenna would have been proud.

"Well . . . if thou must, I would advise to edge closer to yon Mount, Dragon. Daima, or Nainya actually, knows your scent, so they should find it easy to track us unto wherever we may tread."

Brenna sullenly took off in the general direction, muttering something about the 'Bloody high and mighty pricks.' Dedira chose to ignore her, following her. He seemed relaxed, but was actually on high alert. The Alliance was crumbling, and open attacks by the opposing side on his kin and allies were not unheard of. He had silently vowed to protect these people, who had had no rhyme nor reason to help him in his gravest hour, but had risked their lives and the collective wrath of the Clan Heads, or at least half of them.

They continued onward, a half hour seeing them to the base of Dragon Mount. They rested, Dedira sitting on his haunches while Brenna simply lay down in the grass. She closed her eyes and listened to the distant calls of eagles, which seemed to congregate around the halfway point of either mountain. Sunlight seemed to glint off their feathers, and she let herself be soothed by the sweet sounds.

She heard a slight sound of footfalls, and looked up to see Nainya padding toward them. He dragged a dead elk towards her, blood still drying around the wound in her neck. He seemed to grin at her, although it may have been simply a trick of the light. Nonetheless, she affectionately ruffed up the fur on his neck. He licked her, getting a little blood and a lot of saliva on her cheek. She playfully batted him away, never losing her smile as she wiped away the liquid on her sleeve. Dedira walked up to them, looking on the elk with a hint of sadness. **"Pray tell, doth thou believe that but a one of these could feed us all? If not, I will gladly wait until reach sanctuary."**

There was a flash of pure light, and there again stood Daima. He was grinning. "No, I expect it to feed you. Flying takes a lot out of a body, after all." It was true; under normal circumstances a Dragon would expect to devour about a dozen elks a week to keep up their strength up for any serious amount of flying, and that was only a stripling such as Dedira. Dedira bowed his head in thanks before tearing into the carcass. In a few moments, it was gone except for a few spatters of blood to disturb the pristine grass that they sat on.

As soon as he was finished, Daima strode past the dragon, saying, "C'mon you two, we must get there soon, or there'll be hell to pay!" Brenna followed, and Dedira soon after, he being much refreshed by the quick meal. They all didn't bother looking up the mountain that they had to traverse on foot, even if only half way. It was all a bit much to contemplate right then. Reytha remained resolutely out cold.

Daima held up his arm, fist closed and his other gripping the hilt of his sword tightly, so much so that his knuckles had turned white. Brenna failed to notice and might have walked into him if Dedira hadn't suddenly curled his prehensile tail protectively around her, bringing her behind him so that his body shielded her from the steep mountain side that they had been walking side on to. It rose up almost thirty feet from the path that they tread with care, as a sheer drop and a rather horrific and particularly gruesome death awaited them if they happened to slip. She beat on his tail, shouting, "Let go of me, you useless lump! I said—" She was cut off when he moved his tail far enough so that she could see the top of the wall. She had to stifle a scream.

Above them, from the thirty foot precipice stood at least a score of hippogriffs and griffins. The former had the legs and tails of horses, but the upper bodies and wings of eagles, while the later looked similar except for the fact that they had a lions fore legs, and they were bigger. Much bigger. At least two times as large as the hippogriffs, which were half and again the size of a regular horse. Large, to say the least. And they didn't look particularly happy to see them there. In fact, they appeared positively angry.

They shrieked at them, creating a cacophony of horrid sounds that no man has ever heard and lived to tell of. Dedira was un-intimidated by it all, and reared himself to his full height, somehow managing to keep Reytha balanced near his shoulders. He stretched out his neck until he was almost nose to nose with them. He hissed at them, a low sound that seemed to pierce the soul more than the ears and mind. The griffins started flapping their wings, little gusts of wind seeming to form their. They held the power of a windstorm in their wings. The hippogriffs continued to shriek ineffectually, either too stupid or too brave to back down. Or, possibly, both.

Either which way, the Griffins continued to gather wind to them, and Dedira breathed in deeply, prepared to set fire to them, feathers and all. Neither side seemed to be cowed . . . until there was an even higher pitched shriek from behind them. They all of them turned to see a majestic creature flying towards them . . . a phoenix. Fire seemed to radiate from it, giving it the aura of a small sun. It screeched at them again, looking each and every one of them in the eyes. Even the hippogriffs seemed scared of it. Another shriek, and they scattered, the griffins herding their charges back to their nests. The phoenix landed where they had just been, seeming to smile at them. Its head was plumed, and three long, graceful tail feathers lay delicately behind it. Dedira bowed his head in thanks, and the phoenix bowed back. It then flew down to where Reytha still slept fitfully on Dedira's back. Bowing its head one last time, the phoenix let a single tear drop from its beautiful cheek, and it landed on the stricken Kitsune's brow. Then, it flew off, cawing again at them all, leaving a fiery trail in its wake. **"Fare thee**

well, child of the sun." Dedira loosened his grip on Brenna, and Daima released the magical energy he had been building up to combat the griffins. They all three of them heaved a sigh of relief.

Then, Reytha started to stir.

"Is it done?" The great Wyrm, easily three stories high at the shoulder, sat close to a human woman, who had the look of someone who knew how to disappear without anything more than a cloak and a smile. She was clad in full black: black cloak, black leggings, black shirt, and hair died an unnatural looking black, seeming to devour the light around it.

She smiled, showing white teeth in a startling contrast to her attire. "Yes, Liege. The Dragons have not a clue, and the army of Men is ready to move into the Tasavalh Plains, not but a few days from here."

A deep laugh made a report around her, filling the large chamber that this false god called home. *"As I expected of thee, Eileen. I take it that thou hast but a few more nights needed to prepare?"*

Eileen momentarily bit her lip slightly, the only forewarning that she had bad news. "Well . . . we may need more time, Sire. Humans will not move quickly unless you sour them on with greed or pain, and both can only hold for but a little."

"How much time do you need?" The voice held a threat of untold horrors to the woman before Him. She gulped before answering, showing fear that she didn't really feel; she knew that he needed her more than she needed him. Still, sometimes it is best to appear cowed by ones superiors, as there were many things that could happen before death.

"As much as you can buy for us. As I have said, humans are so hard to work with."

He contemplated for a moment, creating a void in the conversation, and an ear-splitting silence all around, seemingly only broken by the erratic breathing of its two occupants. Finally, He stated, *"But a month I can give you, and maybe less, but no more. The beasts cry for battle, and very soon we must oblige them. The elves and dwarves also, they hunger for this impossible war, and most half elves with them. I am glad that thou hast chosen to cooperate with us, Eileen. But a month, but no more can I give unto thee. I do not control them all, and I can only stop them for so long."*

Eileen gave him a thankful smile and bowed to the great beast before her. "I thank thee, Sire; a month is more than enough for our ends."

"As thou wilst, and as thou were." Another smile hid, another bow given in mock politeness.

Fool. *'All is going as you have predicted, Mistress.'*

"Ah, ah . . . good, my child. We shall have our vengeance upon these monsters, for what they have done."

'Thank you. Thank you for choosing me for this. I am honored, truly I am.'

"You are the best, Precious, you always were. Come home; the pawns will do all of our work for now."

'As you will, Mistress.' She turned back to the Wyrm Lord, almost as if she had forgotten something. "Oh, Liege . . . might I borrow one of your subjects? To bring me out of this place unseen, of course."

"Take Rechva, he is swift and may fly far with but a little weight such as thee, Eileen. Speed on, return to thy Master, the King of Men, and send him my regards, and my thanks. All is as planned."

"Of course, Liege. A thousand thanks to thee, and may your wings stay strong and your claws sharp." She turned to leave, but suddenly a large foot in front of her, with claws that easily were as tall as she.

"Remember, Halfling: If you fail in this, than thy punishment will send thee to Hell where thou may believe it to be Paradise, after what I and my subjects have done unto thee. Remember this, and work all the more diligently for it."

"Of course. Fare thee well, oh Lord of Wyrms." He merely went back to a corner of His room, curling up in sleep.

She smiled as she went outside, the cool of the mountain air feeling refreshing to her senses. She mounted the Wyrm that was already there for her, still smiling.

Fools, all of them. She tucked her jet black hair back behind her pointed ears, wishing that all of this would move a bit faster.

They passed on through the mountain the rest of the uneventfully. Reytha was already back on her feet, feeling better than when she had gained her seventh tail. She was smiling and chatting lightly with Brenna about nothing in general. Daima led in front, and Dedira brought up the rear. The dragon was visibly relaxing as he neared his Liege, and that was transmitted to the rest of the group. Daima carried the remaining pack easily, not really worried about the lack of food, or all of their growling stomachs.

Quite all of a sudden, a large opening appeared before them, stretching wide and tall enough to accommodate ten dragons of Dedira's stature to walk abreast. Dedira roared his happiness, Daima cheered slightly, and Reytha hugged Brenna jubilantly, who just wondered why everyone was suddenly making all of this racket on a mountain that was not the best place to be on. Daima led the charge forward, Reytha clasped Brenna's hand and dragged her along, and Dedira lumbered forward at a slightly more sedate pace. This, of course, led them into complete and total darkness, which was made all the more oppressive by the fact that there was a deafening silence surrounding them, seeking to drown them as easily as the oceans could and would to them.

Reytha started to form the magical energy necessary to make a fire, but Daima stopped her, then did it himself.

She put her hands on her hips and stuck her tongue out at him childishly. "Ag, old stick in the mud!"

He commented over his shoulder, "Well, for someone who is a millennia old, you don't seem to have matured, or gained any wisdom or intelligence either!"

She made an "AH!" sound, huffing a little in indignation, although it was all in good fun. He chuckled at her before turning back to light the way for them, although had a sinking feeling that it was mostly for her benefit. She hated being a burden. Daima trudged on ahead, until he stopped at what appeared to be a vast space of stone, exactly like the rest of the tunnel or whatever the hell it was that they were in. He smiled before shifting to Nainya, who sat on his haunches and howled loudly into the oppressive nothingness, plunging them into darkness.

Brenna stood still, suddenly remembering that she had a slight fear of the dark. Abruptly, a slight glow came from ahead . . . or wherever it was that she was looking. It grew in size and intensity until she could make out a torch. It was carried by a tall, graceful looking man, full of youth and beauty. An Elf, it would seem, by his sharply pointed ears, more so than Brenna's by far. He didn't necessarily smile, but he seemed to radiate more light off of his skin than the torch. "Who are you to enter here? By whom are you sent, and on what Errand do you arrive?"

Reytha stepped up, letting all of her tails fan out in plain view. "We are travelers, here to respond to the Gathering that has been announced, and we come of no will but our own. And, nice to see you again, Fahrirh. How long has it been?"

The elf smiled at her. "Ah, Reytha. I believe . . . two centuries? Or was it three? I can't remember as well as of late, as there isn't much to worth remembering. But, who is this? I recognize Daima, the Naish, and Dedira the youngling, but who is this? If I could not see her ears, I would have mistook her for a human."

Reytha used two of her tails to nudge the girl forward, until she was almost face to face with Fahrirh. "This is Brenna, a half-elf, although she was raised as a human. She is here to have Judgment Passed on her." Brenna looked at her friend sharply; she had heard of no such 'Judgment'. This was new and rather disturbing news. Gathering her wits, she bowed to the tall elf, who smiled slightly and bowed back.

It showed true the sword on his back. He straightened, and waved his torch about for a moment. It seemed that, in the space of a second, a thousand more torches were lit all around the room. They saw several elves standing along the low wall by them, arrows still nocked to strings, although they were relaxed at the moment.

Fahrirh made a sweeping motion, eyes sparkling in the torchlight. "Come, come, friends! Erodor has told us of your plight, and food and drink are set out for all of you. Follow me!" He led them away from the Elven archers, and, when Brenna looked back, darkness was cast behind them once again.

Fahrirh led them through another low tunnel, although it was lit by a light all its own. Dedira's head was bowed down, so that his nose was almost at Daima's back. The four of them walked abreast, with the Dragon behind them. Fahrirh talked animatedly with Reytha, the two of them rapidly catching up on the time that they were apart. The two old friends seemed to know the maze of tunnels by heart, and Daima didn't really seem lost. Brenna made sure to keep one hand on his shoulder, in case she got lose, which would not do in such a large place.

When they stopped, she almost went onwards, except Daima caught her, pulling her in to his chest as a sheer drop awaited her had she taken but another step. She blushed despite herself, feeling the heat most about the newly acquired tips of her ears. She quickly pulled away, and he only coughed and fidgeted a bit. Brenna looked anywhere but at him, and noticed the conspicuous lack of a bridge across the gap, which spanned about a hundred yards across. "Um . . . did we, maybe, take a wrong turn?"

"No," was the simple reply from the elf, and it had the immediate effect of making her feel like an idiot (luckily, elves have a habit of making everyone else feel like complete idiots as well, so she was not left out). "We have more protection here than any could guess. This is one of them. If you'll pardon me for a moment . . ." He took first one quick step, than another, and then broke into a sprint, and when he arrived at the edge he jumped far, but not far enough. As he started to plummet, the edge of the other side seemed to reach out and grab him, making itself reach out until it was under his foot. It seemed like he only needed to jump a few feet, not the hundred or so yards that the chasm most certainly spanned. Brenna gaped at him from across the way, and was nudged by Reytha.

"Come on, give it a go!"

Brenna looked at her as if she had grown another seven heads to match her tails. "But . . . but, but, but . . . I can't, you don't . . ."

Of course, she now felt even more of an imbecile, but that was to be expected. Today was, simply put, not her day at all. She shook her head to rid it of all the swirling, confusing and useless thoughts that plagued it. She then folded her arms, showing that stubborn streak that all humans possessed. "No!"

Reytha smiled in the way a mother would smile at a child who was refusing to take their medicine. "Alright then . . . watch me!" Immediately, she took a running leap, and again the ground reached out and caught her. Brenna gaped again, and then decided that she had had enough of being made a fool of, even if it was unintentional. She began her sprint, building up speed and jumping, closing her eyes . . .

Nothing happened. She opened them to reveal herself o the other side, bearing a rather confused look to the two in front of her. She heard a soft thump as Daima leapt across, and a larger one as Dedira simply stepped over the barrier. "Huh?"

Reytha smiled widely at her. "Old Magic, Dear. No one really knows how it works; only that it does. Don't ask too many questions, or you may just get an answer."

"Uh . . . right . . ." She stood up a bit shakily, casting one last look at the gorge, which remained stubbornly at a hundred yards. They all started off once again, following the elf through increasingly widening corridors, so much so that Dedira could have unfurled his wings and flew down them if he had had a mind to. Eventually, after traversing a few more clever traps, they had arrived. Daima smiled wolfishly. He was home.

"She is a good girl, no matter what. And, you can't say that you can't put a Dragon Tamer to good use."

Reytha and Daima, with Dedira at their side, stood bravely before Six of the Twelve. Fafnir, Lady of the Dragons lay before them, head turned so that she could gaze upon them more easily. Her eye was easily as wide as a man was tall, and her teeth were as long as a mans arm reached full. Truly, a fierce Queen for her people. Although her mouth seemed not to move, her voice rose easily to shake the roof.

"That was never my problem, pray tell, I wondered merely if thy companion could be trusted. Was she not, of due course, raised by Humans?"

"But, she is a Half-Elf, and—" Daima was cut off by Brithal, Lord of Foxes.

"We get that, Daima. But, she was raised AS A HUMAN, and she was taught to fear us, AS A HUMAN. Should she not be treated with due caution?

This is one of our last strongholds, and if it were to be known . . . well, we'd be screwed, to put it lightly."

Reytha bowed to him, before speaking again, careful not to stare at his manifold tails that lay gracefully behind him. "What my friend is trying to say, Liege, is that we have been around her for several days, and she seems sincere. We believe that she can be trusted, and she seems to have embraced her heritage fully, even if she is still adjusting to all these new things."

Getting up from his position lounging on the ground, the Lord of Wolves came toward them. The Great Lunes'Hiul'Sadun, the Moon Shadow. His heads easily came past Dedira's shoulder, and his paws each left a wide mark in the dust of the Ante-Chamber that they had perused for this purpose. He stopped before Daima, and sniffed him curiously. *"Well, Bonder, does not your Brother have some say in this matter?"*

Daima bowed, before saying, "But of course, Lord." Then, a flash of light as he reverted, and left Nainya sitting in his place. The Black Wolf bowed as low as he could to his Lord, then spoke in his own tongue to Lunes.

Reytha listened interestedly to the two, while everyone else feigned indifference; except Dedira, who didn't know what was being said at all. After a few more minutes, the Moon Shadow growled low, as a sign of dismissal, and Nainya let Daima out again, while Lunes went back to his perch near the back. He briefly nodded his approval to the five others, and then rested his great head on his paws.

A Phoenix stepped up to them; his head shining a fiery gold that made the sun seem dim. They averted their eyes, both as a sign of respect, and so that they wouldn't go blind from the light. *"Erodor has told me of this girl . . . but he is only a youngling, so I refer to your experience on this matter, Dragon. What say you? None has asked this of you yet."*

Dedira stole a look at the Lord of all Phoenix, Hyul. He took a deep breath. **"I trust her enough,"** he said simply. Hyul smiled, it seemed, and stepped back from the humbled Dragon.

"That is all I need."

"Do you really trust this girl, my child? Pray tell true in this matter, youngling, and do not let any of thy gratitude towards her cloud thy judgment. Can she be trusted, truly?" Dedira was careful not to look the Lady Fafnir in the eyes, as he was not sure what he would see.

He took another breath, as if to steady his frayed nerves. **"I find her to be as worthy of thy trust as any, my Lady. She has saved my life twice** already, and is of the lineage of Turlin, which makes her doubly so. I would trust my life unto her."

Fafnir raised her eyebrow in slight surprise. Who was this girl to warrant such trust from one of her children in such short a time? She snorted, shifting her great bulk to a slightly more comfortable position. *"Indeed, such a child has not been in these halls for too long a time for me . . . but, she still must take the trials, and, if she should prevail against them, then we may teach her true to her heritage. Alas for us and her, first she must pass trial by all of us . . . I fear that she may cross Graechin, for the Wyrms are a powerful enemy, as we all know by now."*

"LET THEM COME!!!!" A great Boar roared out at them.

A Bear, easily twenty feet at the shoulder, roared in agreement.

Fafnir turned to them, eyes showing an inner fire. *"Danich, Kimirh, stay thy tongues!!! We may be scryed here, and lest thou wish for another war at our time of weakness, then stay thy words for now. War will come . . . but we cannot afford it now. Be still, friends."* Both the Boar and the Bear stood down, eyes cast down to the floor. *"They are too many to be counted, our enemies, both within and from the without. Lest we cause a war on many fronts, we must tread with care. I do not doubt the prowess of our warriors . . . but I do doubt that they can stand against so many for long."*

"Against all odds we have prevailed before, so why not again?" Kimirh, the Celestial Bear, seemed to have a more civil tongue in his head now, compared to his last outburst.

"But not these odds, friend," corrected Hyul gently. *"A long time back, these were our allies . . . our friends, even. And it is hard to strike true at one who you once called friend . . . no matter how long ago."*

"Yes," said Fafnir, her eyes holding a great sadness for all to see. *"I regret my folly each morn, for it has caused so much death . . . unto all of us. Lest we trip again, and set the enemy within our midst to attack, we must look ever to the dawning, and do all we can to survive. We are graced; indeed, to have such as would cleave ever to us, no matter the cost."*

"Yes," rang a somber chorus from Brithal, Lunes, and Danich.

Daima and Reytha looked from one of the great Lords to the next, wondering what exactly had happened, so long ago. "And, what of us?" Asked the Kitsune gently to her Liege.

Brithal looked to Fafnir, who nodded her enormous head once. He sighed, as if weary of the world. Maybe he was. He looked Reytha in the eyes, and the Eight tails nodded sadly. So, it was to be done. She looked first to one of her companions, then the others, and no words needed to be passed to tell of them the doom that awaited the girl that they had come to call friend, daughter, savior.

Turning on their heels, they all three of them left from whence they came.

*   *   *

Herold seemed non-pulsed as the Phoenix gracefully glided between the two of them, although Brenna jumped a bit. The sad part was that she wasn't really that surprised at it: The people here seemed to make a habit of surprising her. She sighed and looked closely at the Phoenix . . . well, as close as she could without blinding herself. Being made of a pure flame had that effect on folks.

She did not know him well. That was to say, Herold. He was introduced to her by Reytha, who was rapidly becoming her best friend (even if she was, technically, dead). Either or, Herold was good with a blade, which she desperately needed to work on. The Resistance wouldn't baby anyone; either you pulled your own weight or you could get the Hell out.

"Hey, I know you! You're that Phoenix, from the gorge with the Griffins! You saved us there. Thanks for that, by the way."

"No thanks are necessary. My name is Erodor, of the Clan Phoenix." He made a bow that one would think impossible to do. Brenna noticed that no heat seemed to emanate from the flames that permeated his skin.

She bowed to him. "Brenna . . . Adun'Kial. Yes, that's it. I'm still getting used to all this."

"No problem at all." He turned to Herold, who nodded nonchalantly in Erodor's general direction. "Morning, Elf."

"Damn overgrown sparrow." The two glared at each other a moment before bursting out into laughter.

Brenna looked confusedly at the two, and Herold told her, "Inside joke, I'll tell you later."

"Indeed. So, Herold, you taking her on a grand tour?"

"Yeah, I figured she deserved it, for whatever Hell she was put through. It was worse for me, as no one even knew me, or wanted to. Least I can do for a friend."

"How long ago did you come here, anyway, Herold?"

He grinned. "Twenty three years ago next month."

"Ah." She didn't even bother to be surprised.

"C'mon, there's something that you should see." She followed him down a low hill, gazing worriedly at the large creatures that had taken to the skies here.

Still, she found it hard to worry all that much, out here. This side of Dragon had much more greenery than the side that she had climbed. Trees dotted the place far and wide, with tops of green and white and yellow. Herold led her along a twisting, yet easily traversed, path, well worn and beaten earth crunching slightly beneath her feet. He took her hand when she stumbled on a hidden rock, and Erodor swooped a little lower from his position above them, wings flapping every few seconds.

"You alright?" His eyes held true worry for her.

"Yeah, I'm fine. Let's go see this . . . whatever it is." He nodded to her, and they started up again as Erodor flew back to his previous position. She didn't stumble any longer. They went on for a few more minutes, until Herold stopped in front of a great white topped tree. He smiled at her, and she gaped at the huge monster of a tree, easily ten times her height. "What is this . . . thing . . . ?"

Herold's smile widened, just a little bit. "This is the Mother of all the Kana trees. It is said that She was born of Gevorh himself, when he bled for the sins of Elves, Dwarves, and Men."

"What? Who—" He cut her off with his next speech.

"The Kana trees, they are immortal. A leaf, even separated from the tree, will never wilt. They remain white all through the year, in Winter, in Summer, in Spring, in Fall. They are . . . they are just . . . the Kana trees. They are unexplainable to anyone, even the Lords of the Mountains. And, they only grow here, where Gevorh's love is still strong enough to be felt."

"Okay, thanks for that, but . . . who is Gevorh? Another God, like the Lords?"

Herold chuckled at her, and watched as Erodor landed gracefully on one of the manifold branches of the Mother Kana tree, being careful as to not set fire to the leaves, although they could not actually catch a fire, by their look. "The Lords are not God's at all. In fact—"

He was interrupted as a flame burst through the mountain top, and Mount Dragon seemed to live up to its namesake. Herold paled, and Erodor finished his sentence. "In fact, we have to leave, Brenna, because you seem to have a meeting with those same Lord's we just mentioned. Joy and Rapture galore, eh?"

"Yeah," she said, a little dazed and still recovering from looking at the immense inferno that easily broke through the stone fortress. "Joy and Rapture galore."

She felt as if a million eyes all bored down upon her, ready to crush her soul with their hate and malice. It was disconcerting, to say the least. And, she was not that far off. A million eyes *did* look upon her scrutinizingly, but only half of them wished upon her a painful death. The rest merely wondered if the rumors were true. Arranged around her were every single one of the people and beasts of the Wold that were in this entire Mountain range, numbering in the hundred thousands, at least. The Lords and Ladies sat around her, making good use of the gigantic ledges that were in abundance here. Around them sat their subjects, all of them making some sort of noise, until howls, growls, and screams filled the air.

On the ground level sat the people, the Elves, Half-Elves and Dwarves, and the Men that had deemed this cause worthy of their death, the Hunter tribes that lived near the Forest edge, near the Great Seas. And, in the middle of the vast theater that was her doom, stood Brenna, all alone and scared.

She looked around her, trying to make out the faces of the few friends that she had managed to make in her short time here. The Kitsune's were all on the higher levels, but she thought that Reytha was waving at her. Wolves she could not make out as easily, as they all were of a great multitude of colors, their coats blending with the rocks. Phoenixes and Dragons were on the highest levels, and she knew Herold was with the Half-Elves, who sat a little away from where the other High-Elves glared hatefully at them, although she did not know why.

She jumped as a Wyrm, no more than three feet long, buzzed by her, making its way quickly up to the highest level, where the Dragons and Wyrms resided. She let out a breath and glared after it. Suddenly, an all consuming voice, cold as ice and rough as jagged stone, rang out from above, shaking her to the very core of her being. It was the voice of Graechin, Lord of Wyrms.

"Lest mine eyes deceive me, child, thou hast come here for trial? To seek a place amongst us? To become . . . one of us, doth thou not?"

She nodded her head vigorously. "Yes, sir, Lord Wyrm, sir!" She squeaked it out, and it caused another cacophony of laughs and derisive howls from all the Beasts of the Wold. She blushed a bit, despite herself.

A calmer, more soothing voice came next, and it reminded her of Dedira. *"Fear us not, child of Turlin . . . we seek thee not in dishonor, nor in vengeance or hate. We only wish to see if thou could be trusted well, so speak to us true, Halfling. We will see if thou are worthy of OUR trust, first. Brenna'Adun'Kial, step forward, and may thy heart be steadfast and thy soul true."*

A new voice rang out, and she could see all of the Kitsunes jabbering from above, although she knew not their tongue. She looked up and saw that Brithal spoke, in a voice more calm than Fafnir's. *"C'mon, you two, you're scaring her! Listen, Brenna . . . we only want to ask you a few questions, and see how you answer them. Now, answer each of them truly, yes?"* She nodded dumbly, too stupefied to speak. A Kitsune was one thing, but this . . . this blew her mind. The Great Fox smiled, and then growled out to one of his people. She saw that all of the Lords and Ladies of the Wold did likewise, and she saw a representative from the Elves, Dwarves, and Men step up, although no Half-Elf came, for they were too few to make any real difference.

Abruptly, she found someone hugging her, and turned to find Reytha smiling at her. She embraced her friend, and looked over the others. Dedira was there, as was Fahrirh, and that was the only ones that she knew. Besides them, there was defined looking old Dwarf, who looked at each and every one of them warily. A Wyrm, easily matching Dedira in size, if not wit, perched on a rock nearby, growling at the Dragon, who hissed back obligingly. A wolf, slightly smaller than Nainya, but with a slight bluish tinge to his coat, sat nearby, gazing at them with old, wise eyes. An eagle and a Phoenix, whom she had never seen before, slowly spiraled downward, and a Griffin clawed the ground nearby. Dedira moved closer to her, as he did not at all like the vibes that he was getting from some of the people. A Bear and Boar lay on the dusty Earth near them, and a Leopard dozed across from them. An elk eyed warily the Hunter, an immense black skinned man who looked as if he could kill it bare-handed. A horse galloped around them, burning off some extra energy. Very high strung creatures, horses.

She sat down, cross legged in the middle of it all and simply waited for whatever it was going to be to start. After a few more minutes of everyone jabbering (hissing, growling, braying, and screeching) at each other, it all settled down to where the fifteen representatives sat around her in a circle, with her in the middle. Reytha leaned in closer, as to whisper in her ear. "This is how it works: We all ask you one question each, and you answer them as best you can. Then, each one decides whether or not that you are trust worthy. Basically, it all comes down to the Elves, Dwarves, and Men, who hold no allegiance to Fafnir or Graechin. Impress them to your side, and you're in!"

"And if I don't?"

The Kitsune stayed silent a moment before answering in an undertone, "that will be decided later . . . if you don't get in the first time, that is!" She finished with a false hope that even a blind man could see. Reytha leaned away, a frown almost reaching her face, although she could not hide it from her eyes. A Leopard coughed good naturedly in her direction, licking his paw to remove some invisible dust there.

"Hello there! Mind telling me what your name is, love?" He sounded like a person from Dunland, of all things. Brenna gazed in admiration at his white and black speckled coat before answering.

"Brenna'Adun'Kial, at your service!" She got up and bowed to him, causing the Leopard to chuckle.

"Oh, a gentlewoman! Well, if we go by formalities . . ." He stood up, and placed his foreleg out, doing a fair imitation of a courtly bow to her. "I am Julius, Leopard and Warrior, at *your* service, Brenna."

A Wyrm roughly pushed him aside. **"Grrr, pray tell, Julius! Lest we fall victim to affection for this . . . Half-Breed! Stay thy tongue, and keep thyself away from her!"** Julius turned from her, shamefaced. Brenna fought down the urge to feel sorry for him. He would only vote against her, anyway. The Wyrm turned to her, pushing his foul head close, so that she turned her head as to not breathe in his stench, caused, no doubt, by some poor creature rotting in the back of his throat. **"Now, Halfling, I've but a question to ask of thee. Wilst thou answer me?"** She nodded her head, not trusting to open her mouth and not vomit all over the stone floor. **"Good. Now . . . why art thou here, in this, our home? What right hast thee to defile this place, wench?"**

Dedira placed himself between the two, roaring out a challenge to the Wyrm. Brenna touched his shoulder, and that simple act bid him calm almost immediately, although he still glared hatefully at the Wyrm. Brenna stepped out from behind him. "I came because . . . I realize now that humans have no right to file everything away under some category, to list everything as one thing or the other. My eyes are opened, and they shall not be closed again to this. The wonder in the world shall stay . . . and I will help it."

The Wyrm backed down, not expecting such an eloquent answer from the girl of scarcely sixteen years of age. A Boar stepped up beside her, snorting a little bit as he gouged the dust and dirt with his tusks. "Alright, girl . . . what caused you to come? We know why, but what 'opened your eyes', as you call it?"

Brenna sighed a bit, knowing this wasn't going to end soon enough for her liking. "I guess . . . Daima. When he came, and fought that . . . whatchamacallit, I forget the name . . . but, he told me that the time for a Damsel in Distress was gone, and I would have to learn to fend for myself if I wanted to survive. Also, that caused my ears to grow in," she finished, flicking the points of her ears for emphasis.

Smiling, she made ready to answer the question from the Bear. "Why did you believe the Naish? I've met this one, and his Bonded . . . why? What did he do to gain your trust?" Her smile disappeared for a moment.

"I don't really know. Just . . . cause, well . . . he's the only one who showed me any kindness, even that much. When I worked at the inn . . . I just did it to survive. Everyone there treated me below dirt, just because I looked differently then them. I hated it, and then Daima saved me from being raped, without any thought of a reward. He just did it . . . just like that, without a second thought. Then, he saved me again from the . . . whatchamacallit."

"Were-bear," corrected Reytha. She clapped Brenna on her shoulder. "Good answer, dear." Brenna could only smile and nod her thanks before the next answer came.

It was from the old wolf. He panted a little bit, even in the cool air of the mountain interior. "So . . . young pup, what have you to say on what you think of us?"

"Huh?"

A low growling sound came from the oldster's throat, which Brenna could only place as a chuckle. "What do you think of all this, the Mountain, and Wold, and your heritage?"

"Oh! It's all great. I never knew anyone like a mother—" here, Reytha winced a bit "—but, I think that this is the best thing that's ever happened to me, personally. And, everyone here, they're so . . . amazing!" She was caught up in the exuberance of a child, which she still was, by many accounts. "I mean, come *on*!!! All the animals, they talk! Although, I guess you could see that, but . . . still . . . Elves! Dwarves! Talking Foxes! And . . . and . . . oh . . ." She blushed and sat down when she realized how childish she must have sounded to them. Said beasts and man and significant others laughed at her expense, but not cruelly. Well, the Wyrm did, but that was expected.

Abruptly, the happy mood ceased as the Phoenix stepped up, landing just before the eagle did. "For whom would you die for?"

Brenna had the were-withal not to seem taken aback by the abrupt seriousness, but still stumbled over her words. "I . . . I would die . . . for my friends, and . . . for anyone here, I guess." She fought down a wince as the last two words slipped out, but no one seemed to care.

"For whom would you kill for?" The eagle's voice seemed to come from right beside her ear, even though he was standing across from her.

"The same people," she answered, this time with more firmness.

The eagle *kreed* out, then took off into the air again, as anyone who could take to wing would prefer it to walking. The horse cantered up to her, slowing to a stop mere inches from where she stood. "And what of you, child?" She asked it in a cultured, motherly voice, something that Brenna had not expected from the hyperactive beast. "Would you die for yourself? Would you kill for yourself?"

Brenna could not cover her surprise at the question, which showed the true depth of her dumbfounded ness: she had learned to not be too surprised anymore by what she saw, as she had seen and heard too much as it was. "I . . . I don't know. Does anyone ever?" She tried to sound wise with the question she nailed on to the end, but only succeeded in making herself seem an idiot with delusions of wisdom.

The horse nickered, and took off, probably to do some more laps around the circle of animals and people. Dedira looked sadly at her, eyes full of pain for her plight. **"What dost thou believe of battle, dear-heart?"** He probably wanted to give her an easy question, but this one stumped her. After a moment, she answered.

"I'm okay with it . . . I guess. That is, if its for the right reasons." Close shave. Too close.

Dedira sighed heavily, and lay down next to Reytha, who looked as stressed out as he did. All that were left to question her were the Griffin, Elk, Reytha, the Hunter, the Elf, and the Dwarf. Oh, Rapture. The Griffin launched himself over her head, wings splayed, as if to impress her. He skidded to a stop nearby, and walked back to her. "What weapons can you use, and how well?"

"Well, I can use the bow, and am pretty good at that. But, besides that, I never had a chance to use anything else, so we'll just have to see about that!" She crossed her arms and looked him in the eyes, until he backed down. But, her hackles were still raised from the contest of wills.

"Alright, Dear . . . what do you believe when it comes to magic?" Good, an easy one! Finally!

"Well, I'm fine with it. In fact, it is a big help to most everything I can think of, so I think that more power to whoever can use it."

"Can you use magic at all?" The Elk hadn't even missed a beat.

"Uh . . . no, but I can learn it." Her shoulders sagged just a little bit at the weakness evident in her voice.

All that was left were the Elf, Dwarf, and Man. The giant black-skinned one stepped up, walking closer until he was almost nose to nose with her. In his deep, deep voice, he asked, "Can you hunt?" Figures.

"If I have to." Curt question, curt answer. But, the thing that unnerved her the most was his eyes. They never left her own, and she knew that you can see the lie in someone's eyes. He didn't smile, or even deem to say anything else. He simply stepped back, letting Fahrirh take his place. The Elf seemed to smile at her, although it could be a trick of the lighting.

"Tell me, Brenna . . . do you know anything of the Elves, who are half of your lineage?"

She could not meet his eyes as she ground out, shame faced, "No." That was all that the High-Elf needed as he stepped away from her, letting the Dwarf take his place.

He was a stocky fellow, with a magnificent beard of silver strands, making him almost two hundred, as a Dwarf would never cut his beard off in any way at all. His voice, when he spoke, was rough and gravely, but not in an unpleasant way. More like Granddad would sound. "Well, girl . . . I can't say that I'm disposed to ye, but I'll give ye a try. What do you believe as to God's?"

She screwed up her face in concentration for a moment. Then, she said, "Well, I believe that *something* is out there, looking out for us, although I'm not sure who. I like to think that there is something after death, although I wouldn't know, as I haven't died yet." The Dwarf smiled, and bowed low, his nose almost touching the ground.

Reytha sighed happily. "Good answer, dear," she whispered. But, there was no time for any niceties, as all of the animals and people surrounding her suddenly left for their respective leaders. They started to converse in small voices, filling the high anti-chamber with a low rumbling sound. She could only sit dejectedly on the floor and wait for the dreaded verdict to come. After a few minutes, the room quieted down enough to allow for some individual voices to be heard.

However, all were silenced as Fafnir roared out for silence, allowing for no extra words to be thrown about in the already volatile situation. ***"SILENCE!!!!!! I said . . . BE QUIET!!!!!!!!"*** The remaining voices died away in fear of the Great Lady of the Fire Drakes. ***"Now . . . the verdict from the Clans."*** One by one, the expected answers from those under the allegiance of Fafnir and Graechin came, namely For and Against, as expected. ***"Now, the Verdict of the Houses."***

This was the part that really counted for her, as these three votes could decide whether or not she would be able to stay. If not . . . well, that was to be decided. First came up the Humans. The same man who had asked her whether or not she could hunt stood, going a little out to be better heard. His voice, even when shouting, was low, but commanded a presence. "We say . . . let her be!" An immediate jabbering came from the Elves, who looked displeased. Fahrirh stormed out of the pulpit that housed the Elven brethren. Brenna was close enough to hear there heated words to one another.

"What are you doing, Kahn? You would suffer this . . . *half-breed* . . . to live?"

"I care not for what she is or was, only who she is as herself." Kahn's voice held seemingly infinite wisdom in it, evenly matching the up until now unflappable Fahrirh.

"But she is an abomination! She should not be allowed to exist! It is bad enough that there are so many of the bastards about already, and you want *more* to defile this place?"

"You forget your place Elf," ground out the Human, voice dripping venom. "Your narrow-mindedness will haunt you all to the end. Or, do you not remember that hate is the reason that we are fighting a war to the death?"

Fahrirh did not allow himself to lose any anger. "But this is different! She is a *half-breed*! A monster!"

"Your words remind me of another, who bespoke of uniting all men together, only to kill off all those who looked different from he." Kahn jerked his thumb back to the wall in a general easterly direction, where the Kingdom of Men lay. Fahrirh's eyes glowed menacingly as he rose to his full height. Kahn was no fool, and surely knew that, even though he was a very strong man, he was no match for a High-Elf, and especially an enraged one. "Sit down, Fahrirh. The vote is cast." Fahrirh didn't take his glare from the man, but finally turned away, pausing to spit on the ground near Brenna's feet.

He yelled out hoarsely to the crowd, "We say let her die!!!!" The Elves cheered their approval; as did a few Dwarves, but those were quickly silenced by their fellows. Brenna's face paled; who knew that she would be hated simply for existing? Silence resumed amongst the gathered throng of people, some who sought her safety, and others who wished her death. So be it.

The same defined looking Dwarf who had been so appraising of everyone stood up, rising only a little from the pulpit where the Dwarves rested. He sighed, and took in a deep breath. "We, in all fairness and justice, are, sadly, finding this girl lacking. We cannot put our trust in someone who lies so easily . . . and so, we cast a vote against her." He turned to her, and she could see the pain in his eyes. He had been outvoted by the Dwarves. "I am sorry, Brenna-dian," he added in an undertone. But Brenna could only hear the voice of Fahrirh reverberating in her mind. *'We say let her die!'*

'She is a half-breed*!'*

'An abomination!'

'A monster!'

'We say, let her die!'

'Let her die!'

'DIE!!!!'

Her world was consumed by those small words that spelled out her doom to all who could see.

She faintly heard the Elves clamoring at the Clan Heads, the illusion of perfection that had so long surrounded them shattered irreparably.

"SILENCE!!!!!" Fafnir held a fire in hr eyes that cowed the Elves. **"This girl shall not be harmed!!! She came here in good will, and shall leave here as such!!!!"**

Graechin shook his head, his own voice rumbling across the fastness of the Mountain and down to her easily. *"We can not risk her telling of us here, Lady Dragon. Lest she betray us, should we not seek the sure and true way of this? One who is dead is unable to tell of our secrets—and they are many."*

"And yet I gave her MY protection! She is my charge here, and I will not suffer her to be harmed at all, Wyrm Lord!"

"I believe that it would anger the Elves very much to see her live. Remember well that they make up many thousands in our force, and—"

"And where may be these so-called 'Forces', hmmm!?!?! I see them not!"

"They will be here, in the end." Never once did the Lord of such a volatile race raise his voice above what it was now. *"Wait and see, Lady of the Dragons."*

"I am tired of awaiting for the Elves to mobilize! Surely, such a long lived and 'wise' race should have learned the meaning of haste by now!!! Lest we be stayed in this place for ever, I would see our allies soon! At least, the Dwarves are marching, and many Hunters also are here, but yet, not doth mine eyes see the many thousands upon which the Lord and Lady Elf have sworn unto our noble cause, as I only see this small force of rabble rousers! Surely, are the Elves so narrow minded that they would not suffer one of their own number to live if she were fathered by a son of Gevorh?"

One Elf stood up, and went where Fahrirh had just stood. "She is not one of us," he called out to the Lord and Lady perched atop the highest shelf, his voice resounding out clearly thanks to the way the structure was formed. "She has no place here . . . or anywhere!"

"And yet, you suffer these others to live, so why not another?"

"They have the protection of the Queen Mother!!!" His voice was showing how he thought of that *particular* aspect of the Empire of the Immortals. Namely, he wished it weren't there at all. "She does not!"

"Has yet not," the Nobel Dragon corrected.

"And she will not! They were-unfortunately—born inside of our Kingdom in the Leaves. But she, she is but a Human raised cur!"

"Stay thy tongue of its insolence, whelp! I know of the laws, as I was there when they were set in place! Only I and my brethren Lords have seen with our own eyes the creation of your Empire, so do not mock me with thy spoilt view on such, lest I fall pray to losing my temper!"

Beaten, the Elf bowed. "My . . . apologies, O' Mistress of the Flames. I shall not trespass as such again."

"Get on with it," stated the bored Graechin. *"Like it or no, O' Mistress Fire Drake, thy best efforts cannot save the child from the wrath of the Elves.*

Lest we start a war unto the ends of time with our most powerful allies, let us hastily make amends unto them, as I feel not like taking the blood of the Fair ones so easily. You can do naught here: the girl must die." He said it with the authority of death Himself. Fafnir bowed her head in shamed defeat, realizing that, for this time, the Wyrm was right.

And, as the words resounded around her in a hail of gleeful laughter, Brenna's small, fragile world came crashing down around her shoulders. Then, all was consumed in black and dark . . .

****7****

She came to, slowly, oh so slowly, savoring the warmth that surrounded her like a blanket. When she opened her eyes, she realized that was because it *was* a blanket. Go figure. She kicked it off her grudgingly, not at all liking the feeling of cold and emptiness that came with it. Then, of course, someone was behind her. She realized that, not by any of her (admittedly weak) senses, but when he cleared his throat.

She spun around to see Herold, who was smiling sheepishly at her as he leaned against the stone wall. He wore a homespun tunic the mixed well with the color of the mountain. No wonder she hadn't seen him. "What do you people want with me? You want to scare me to death before that chief Wyrm, whoshisface, decides to take me out the old fashioned way?"

"Sorry," he said tersely. "And it's Graechin, not whoshisface, as you put it."

"Well, I can't really find the energy to care right now, as I am going to *die* in a little while!"

"Um . . . yeah . . . about that . . ."

"What?" She asked guardedly, afraid of committing too much of her already shattered hope. When he didn't answer, she moved on him menacingly, arms raised as if to strangle him. "WELL!??!?!?! WHAT?!?!?!?!"

He ducked under her outstretched arms, his face a mix of terror and amusement. "There may . . . *may* . . . be a loophole, but you'll need to see the Mistress Dragon, in . . . oh . . . *now.*"

She lowered her arms, face going slack in amazement. Then, she threw her arms around the surprised Half-Elf, kissing him soundly on the cheek before running out of the room. He waited there for a minute.

She came back in, arms behind her back, face red from embarrassment. "Err . . . heh heh; you were going to lead the way?"

Smiling, he led the way.

Brenna never realized how *big* the mountain really was, in comparison to everything she'd ever known. Halls upon hallways upon rooms upon rooms carved into the living rock. She had no clue as to how Herold and everyone else didn't get lost in here. "Whoa . . . and every other mountain is carved just like this?"

"Yep . . . each has rooms for every single member of its race, if they need a place to rest. Most opt to go out into the Forest or world at large, but a few hundred always stay in Wold, or at least nearby. It works, although the system could be better."

She ducked under a burning torch, probably lit by Dragon fire. "Wow . . . say, why the big war with Humans? I mean, if each of these guys has such obvious power, why not use it against the humans in the Empire?"

Herold sighed as he led her ever closer to the Lady of Dragons. "It's not so simple, but there are two main reasons. The first is the most practical; they don't want to leave their position open to attack by the other side. You saw how much the Twelve bicker amongst themselves?"

"Yeah, it's kinda hard to miss."

"Well, that's that part. But, the other, and most important, reason, is much more complicated. You see, you have to remember that there was originally only One Lord, Gevorh, who decided to create companions to Him, because He was the only one on the Earth. He created the twelve Lords, and was content for a while. But, He saw that, while He was happy to have the Twelve, they had naught to do. So, He told them to create a race in their image. But they asked of Him if He could make a race of His own, as a sort of contest. So they did, creating the Dragons and Wyrms and all the rest. But, you see, Gevorh was different from they, and He could not get a race to be just right, so He created three. First, the Elves, with His Eternal Youth. Next, The Dwarves, with His Pride and Wisdom. But, when He created the race of Men and Women, He encountered a problem. As you know, the Elves had immortality, and the Dwarves had long life and could take joy in their works. But, the biggest difference 'twixt the three were that the Elves and Dwarves could do magic, of a sort. Humans could not, and add to that that they are the shortest lived of all three. So, He gave them a *special* gift, the gift of Resolve. In simple terms, it means that, as a whole, they have more magic than the Elves and Dwarves combined, if only when all of them have a single goal in mind. That is why we must go to war, for if we were to lay waste to the Empire, the Hunters may turn on us, and we would face their special magic. If all humans willed us away, then we would simply fall into the void of time, replaced by dumb beasts. Also, the Lords have less power than they seem to have. Between you and me, most of it is show and bluff, to cow us into submission. Also, that is why the Elves hate us so; we possess the gifts of both Elf and Man."

"Well, that's . . . interesting . . . say, what happened to Gevorh? Shouldn't He have stopped this by now?" She still couldn't quite believe of an even *more* powerful being than the Clan Heads.

"Oh . . ." Herold's face saddened. "He decided that there was nothing else He could give his children, so He Ascended to Heaven, forfeiting His true Body in favor of one up in Heaven."

"So, He is . . . a *true* God?"

"Yes." He sighed again, more heavily this time. "We need that battle, so that when the Humans lose we can show them mercy."

"If they lose," Brenna corrected.

"*When* they lose," he restated firmly. She decided not to argue the point with the stubborn Half-Elf, and they walked on in silence for a few more minutes until they reached a great doorway. He gave the huge double doors a single knock, and they opened inwards, a great draft exiting, cooling them enough to make Brenna shiver slightly. She stepped in, and was startled when Herold didn't follow. He waved after her solemnly, knowing that this was a one in a million shot that they were attempting. He could only hope that no one would find out, because to interrupt the ceremony was almost certain death for Brenna. He took up his position by the door, sword loosened in its sheath.

Just in case.

A huge feeling rushed up to the girl, its sheer *presence* nearly bowling her over in fear and awe. Two red eyes stared unblinkingly at her, holding infinite wisdom and an even greater sorrow that she couldn't even begin to comprehend. Never before had she been so close to anything with such . . . such *majesty* as Fafnir, Queen of the Fire Drakes. Despite herself, she bowed low to her. The eyes blinked, then moved a little closer.

"Thou hast not any need at all to bow unto me, my child." "Brenna straightened, and nodded at her. **"Lest we tarry ere long here, we must begin. I am told that thou hast saved the life of a youngling under my care, Dedira?"**

Brenna took a moment to decipher the old speech that Fafnir used, as she had yet to get used to it. "Well, I just distracted the Wyrms. Reytha saved him, and Daima did more than I did. I just . . . comforted him, I guess." She had no clue as to what was happening now.

"Tis not as I was told, Dear Heart. Lest we be deceived by our own falsehoods, let us begin here. Do you trust me?"

Brenna didn't take a second to think before answering. "Yes." Fafnir radiated an aura of a mother, someone whom you could confide in easily and not worry about repercussions. Even her voice was soft like a mother's was supposed to be.

"Good. What we have planned here is dangerous, as there is but I to guide the ceremony. I . . . I have gone against the will of the council, and if we were to be found, their reprisal would be swift. And deadly. My compatriots will try to stall them, but they are few and but warriors, not overly versed in the art of statecraft. But, thou should be warned; we were forced to skimp a little on the niceties of this ceremony, so do not act surprised when there are some things which we could not have easily forestalled. My apologies, but quickly now, Child."

"What . . . what are you going to do to me?" There was no fear in her voice, only curiosity.

"She's going to make you into a Naish, Brenna. Consider yourself lucky, not many people have the privilege of a *Dragon* being willing to share their body with you."

"A Naish? Why? How is that going to help me when I am already damned?"

"So many questions! You see, Dear Heart, Graechin and his underlings cannot damn Dedira for being a Half-Elf, or at least not openly. But, I must warn you, you will be plunged into a world such as thou hast never dreamed before. And a dangerous one, at that. Lest we tarry in niceties, I must ask of thee, do you accept this burden?"

"I . . . I . . . yes. I do."

"Good. Follow me, Child, and let us see unto the future!" The eyes, which had only blinked three times during the whole exchange, moved off, and Brenna and Daima followed. She led the two into a (relatively) low room, and all was cast into light. Fafnir sat there in all her glory, trying vainly to fit easily into the room that towered over the others heads. Reytha was there, just finishing a pentagram, the red paint there still wet. Dedira rested nearby. Reytha smiled at her sadly, and beckoned her over.

She sighed unhappily. "Oh, how I wish there was another way!"

"Why? Reytha, what's wrong?"

"You see, dear . . . this is the old magic. The Blood Magic. Its much more powerful, but . . . well, I need your blood for this to work, just as I needed Dedira's. It will hurt . . . a lot." Brenna noticed that, indeed, the so called "paint" was Dragon's blood. She steadfastly proffered her arm, which Reytha gingerly cut into, letting Dedira's blood mix with hers while some pure drops spattered onto the stone floor. Brenna suppressed a shudder, as she always had a slight phobia of seeing blood, especially if it was her own. When it was done, Reytha stepped back, distaste evident on her face. She never did like the Blood ways, they just seemed too . . . barbaric, for her tastes. Still, if it would save the girls life, then she would put her own beliefs aside . . . for now. As she sunk back into the shadows, the Eight-Tailed woman whispered, "Never step out of the lines, or it won't work." Then, she was gone.

Brenna watched as the blood started to be absorbed into the pentagram of blood, and almost jumped when Fafnir called out in a booming voice, *"Daima'udun, step forth and be known!"* He did so, until he was almost nose to nose with Brenna, feet mere inches from the edges of the pentagram. *"By the Will of the Father, be stemmed thy blood!"* Daima muttered a few incoherent words, and the lines of the five pointed star began to glow with an inner fire that did not burn her. *"Reytha, Kitsune-hijude, step forth, and be known!"*

Reytha took her place by Daima, smiling a little bit sheepishly. *"By the Will of the Mother, Let the Fires be Stoked unto Eternity!"* Reytha placed her hands together, and said "Julen!" Immediately, the fires inside burst out, doing as was bid. And, before the world of Brenna'Adun'Kial was consumed in flames and ashes, she heard the call.

"Dedira, son of Aseroth, son of Damigan, step forth and be known! By the Will of the Bonded, let they two be joined in Brotherhood!"

She moaned into the sheets that made an obvious attempt to suffocate her in fluffy goodness. Bastards. She rubbed her aching head, trying vainly to relieve it of the migraine that was slowly building up steam. If she hadn't known better (or if she had a mallet), she'd have split her head open to break the pressure there. As it was, she felt as if her head would burst in two.

"Yes, that's as side affect, Dear One. We should have warned of it, but we had naught but a little time."

"Dedira? Where the bloody Hell are you?"

"Well, thou couldst say that I am you, now, Dear Heart. But, we would be confused, as like as not."

"Make sense, damn you!" She was in no mood for riddles from the oversized lizard. "You Oversized Lizard, make some more coherent answers!"

"You don't remember, love?" She shook her head in confusion. The Dragon sighed, although it seemed strangely close by. *"The Bonding Ceremony, Oh Lady Dragon Tamer! You and I were made one, of a sort. We are Naish now!"*

"Oh! Oh . . ." She looked thoughtful for a moment. *'So, I guess that I should just think to you, now, if I want to speak top you?'*

"Yes, Brenna. And, you are saved . . . of a sort . . ."

'What do you mean, "of a sort"?' She would have eyed him warily, if not for the fact that he was merely a voice inside her head.

"Look at your arm." She tore at her sleeve to reveal . . . nothing. The Dragon sighed. *"Your other arm, Love."*

"Oh," she said aloud sheepishly. She slowly lifted up the sleeve of her right arm. She gasped. A tattoo lay there, a Dragon surrounding a curved sword. The Dragon was breathing fire, and seemed to wink at her every so often. *'What . . . why . . . huh?'*

"The mark of the Naish. It tells true thy Bonder and thy Blade. We must away, unto the smithy. They shall make thee thy blade, lest you be unarmed when they attack."

'Who is" they"?' The poor girl was more than a little confused at all this, but it was rather disorienting to have a Dragon yammering on inside your skull.

"'They' are the Griffins, Eagles, Wyrms, et cetera that call Graechin Liege. They shall call thee their sworn enemy ere this day is out, for they were cheated out of thy execution."

'Well, why the Hell don't the Heads stop all this?'

Dedira sighed at her typical question. *"Tis not a question of why, but if, Dear One. It is partly that they cannot, but mostly that they will not. Tis . . . a competition, amongst they who hold true power, that their underlings should battle in undeclared war, unto death. It is pride that keeps us fighting."*

'That's horrible!'

"And wasteful. But, alas for we, tis too late for the likes of we. Our call is to battle the Empire of Men, and yet we continue to bloody each other in a war that neither wants. We are damned by their Rivalry, and yet we still hold loyalty unto they who would do this. Because, in the end, they are as us."

'Oh, dear. That doesn't sound good at all.'

"Tis not, Love, but no rest for the weary, and no tears over blood long ago spilt. Come, we must away unto the smithy, lest we be caught out here, unarmed. Let me guide thee there, as you doth not know the way."

'Sure, just give me the directions!'

"Ah, but, alas, tis not as simple as that, Love. I know the way only by smell, and not yet hast thy nose begun to change unto the better that would come of our Bonding." Brenna took a moment to decipher this as that he couldn't lead her there if he only remained a voice in her head.

"Oh, Joy," she said aloud. Then, to Dedira, *'How, pray tell, would one let you out?'* She realized that she was starting to talk like the Dragons would. "Oh, Joy," she repeated.

"Simply allow thyself to relax unto the utmost, and let me out. Tis but a simple thing, and I have been trained for it. Alas, no, that you were not told of this until the very last minute?"

"Yeah, yeah, alas and whatnot. Now, relax . . . hmmm, this could pose a problem . . . uh, what is relaxing?" She asked it aloud to the room, and did not expect any answer.

Oh, how Fate loves to mess about with this girl. "Try thinking of wildflowers," said Daima from where he leaned in the doorway. "It always helps me, when I need to Descend."

She jumped up where she had been sitting on the bed. "What the Hell! Haven't you people heard of *knocking*?"

"What's that?" He asked with an innocent expression which bedeviled her to no end. "Either or, try thinking of wildflowers. It sure helped me, and I was more wound up about descending for the first time than you. 'Course, I wasn't condemned to death by a giant not-Fire Breathing Giant Lizard and his cronies. But, then, not many have been."

"Uh . . . *right*. Well, here goes . . . something, I hope." She lay back down on the bed, but Daima coughed rather loudly. She opened her eyes and glared at him. "What?" She ground out.

"You might want to do this outside, y'know? It's kinda hard to get a Dragon out of a door meant for Elves and the like."

"Oh," she said embarrassedly. She shuffled past the veteran Naish and lay outside on what passed for a grassy knoll in this place. She closed her eyes and tried to feel at peace with the world around her. Of course, it is very hard to find peace in the world, even when a group of homicidal Overgrown Lizards *wasn't* out for your very blood and bones. Even then, one cannot simply *feel* at peace, because if you look for peace then you probably won't find it. So, as she was wont to do when bored, she went to sleep.

"Finally! It seemed as ages since last I smelt true air! Daima, I carry new respect towards thee, and even more so unto thy Brother," said the Dragon as he abruptly appeared in the real world. He turned his thoughts inward for a moment, tuning out the still silent Daima. *'Brenna, Love, art thou alright?'*

"Hmmm? What? What the deuce? Where the Hell am I? And why is there so many . . . oh . . . never mind . . ."

The Dragon would have stared at his new Sister (had it not been for the fact that she was merely a voice in his head at the moment. He resorted to ignoring her little comment. *'Right, love, you're in your Dreamscape. When I am out in the World, that is your own little reality, which has whatever thou wishes for there. Your own little world, really. I won't bother asking of thee what is there, as I am sure that I would not wish to know.'* Indeed, human anatomy did not interest him at all.

"Anyway, I am just wondering why there are so many trees here. Can I change that up a bit?"

Ah, so not what the Dragon had first thought. Fair enough for him. *'Just will them to be gone hard enough, and they will be.'*

"Ah. Well, here goes nothing." Dedira felt her concentrating on said trees, so hard that she'd probably make them burst into flames. As if on cue, she yelled out, *"OH SHIT!!!! Damnit, no fires supposed to be in here! Out I say!!!"*

After a moment, she came back into the connection with a heavy sigh. *"Thanks. Why, exactly, was I not told of all this until after the fact? That little trick with the trees would have come in handy, y'know."*

'We were bereft of time, Dear Heart, and feared for thy life. Lest Graechin move upon thy life first, we hastened to bond thee to me. It worked, and any discomfort is worth it.'

"Oh . . . thanks. Say, why is everyone going through this much trouble for me, anyway?"

'I . . . cannot say. Ponder not upon this, for I know not the answer which to give.'

"Liar. You know it!"

'I fear that I do not, Sister.'

"Pah! Don't cut me out of this! Give an answer already!"

'I am bidden against it, for fear of thy health of mind and body.'

"Like Hell you are. Give me an answer or I will poke you and prod you ant not shut up for—" He cut the connection on her, shaking his great head in sadness.

"She is very opinionated and stubborn, my friend," said the Dragon to the Naish before him.

"Yeah, she can be that," he agreed readily. "Still . . . thanks, for all this. I know that it must be hard on you, becoming a Naish. But, you saved her . . . Lilain would have thanked you, so I'll do it for her. Thank you, Dedira."

"**Tis not a problem for such as I. In fact, it is an honor which I shall bear with pride. Tis I who should thank thee, Daima of the Naish . . . Brother.**"

"Bound by blood," began Daima.

"**Bound by battle,**" finished the Dragon. It was a little ritual of the Naish which the Dragons had become fond of. It bound the two in friendship, although it was hardly needed.

"Well, I guess that you should go. Go and get her a sword, and maybe a better bow." He smiled and nodded at the Dragon, who took off into the rosy fingered dawn, to where smoke slowly rose in spirals from his destination.

****8****

Winging quickly towards the far edge of the immense Mountain that many would call Home, the smithy hove into view. It was a small building (compared to the Mountain's immense proportions), but fitted Dedira comfortably enough. He folded his wings and stalked over to a cheery looking blacksmith, who had just finished hammering out a shield for some proud warrior or other. He was a tall, hefty looking half-Elf, ears tapering to a slight point. He smiled when he saw Dedira, as Dragons usually had some sort of gold to give him for whatever bauble it was that they desired. "Hello, sir Dragon! What may I do for you today?"

"Greetings unto thee, Smithy. I am in need of a blade for my Bond Sister, for she is new unto this world of ours. Pray tell, art thou capable of creating the weapon for which was ordained unto her?"

"Well, give me a look at her tattoo, and I'll see what I can do. They usually come by easy 'nough, but it'll cost you."

"How much for but her steel? Also, my friend told me of her prowess with the Box, couldst thou make for her such a weapon as would be fitting of she?"

"I'll give it a look-see, and see what I can do. You'd best let her out, though."

"But of course." He vanished in the threshold of light that heralded a Naish letting loose their other half. Brenna appeared before him, looking slightly dazed. The smith smiled all the more.

He held out his hand, which she shook. "Names Jihael, pleased to meetcha." He gave an awkward sort of bow, crumpling the apron which was stained black from the soot which he constantly worked with. "Here, lass, let me take a look-see at your tattoo, mayhaps I can try my hand at making it, and that Bow a yours." He took her proffered arm, moving the sleeve up a little to unveil the tattoo that marked her as a Naish. He frowned at the look of it; the curved blade surrounded by the Dragon.

Not quite a scimitar, but definitely not a broadsword, probably perfect for someone of her build. He sighed, thinking of how this would cut into his free time, if he wanted to do a decent enough job. "This'll cost you, maybe three pounds in gold for the sword alone. Then another one and a quarter for the bow, if'n you still want it after this."

"I guess . . . wait, I don't have any gold at all! And where do you get off, selling a sword for *three pounds of gold*?"

"It's a very good sword," he said meekly.

"But soft, for he speaks true! Brenna, Dear Heart, that sword which lies upon thy arm, tis a work of great craftsmanship which would tax the efforts of even a smith as great as Jihael. As for the gold, tell him to take it from the Lady Fafnir. She hath left unto us a little gold for thee, enough for the sword and bow. If tis too much, then I have but a little to spend with thee for thy arms."

'No! Its my things, you shouldn't have to waste money on me!'

"Thou forgets, Dear one, tis my skin, too, which shall be defended by thy blade and bow. Now, tell him of these new tidings, and let him get on with his job."

She turned back to Jihael, who seemed to realize that she had been conversing with her Bond-Brother. His expression clearly said 'So? What next?' She smiled sheepishly. "Um, right . . . Dedira says that you should take the gold from the account of the Lady Fafnir, and his if it is not enough. When should I come back for the sword and bow?"

"I'll have blade, bow, and a quiver of arrows ready for you three days hence. 'Till then, have fun." He waved her off, and she took that as her cue to leave. She thought about lazing about in wildflowers, and soon found herself in a large field of them, as she went into the dreamtime as Dedira took to wing. It was much more pleasant than the real world.

*   *   *

"Are you sure? Could she really be the one?" Graechin asked worriedly.

"Aye, I am sure of it. She has the blasted 'Tamers blood in her," replied the Griffin Lord, Kaiden. Great, feathery wings rested upon his back. *"Its true, I fear, and we cannot stop it."*

"She is sentenced to death now! What, truly, could my nemesis do unto our true meanings?"

"She is Naish now," said the great Lord almost meekly (it is hard to be meek when one is two stories at the shoulder). He winced as Graechin howled in rage, his great claws gouging furrows into the old stone.

"WHAT?!!?! How could this be? I shalt not suffer this injustice, this . . . this DISGRACE unto my name!!! She shall DIE!!!!!"

"As you say," stalked up the Clan Head of the Leopards, Polious Regla. The snow white cat stood defiantly before the only one upon this Earth that could cow him. *"But, she will be protected. And, why, exactly, do we fear her?"* They did not so much speak as project their thoughts.

"I fear none! But, alas, she is destined to unite the clans—under the rule of Dragon! It shall ruin us all!" The great statesman who had been shown during the hearing was gone, replaced by the pure, primal beast which he truly was. *"They shall seek out the Humans and battle them for past injustices—such is the way unto ruin! I shall not allow us to fall!"*

"But, if it is destined, would killing her really stop it?"

"Naught is set in stone, Leopard King. Surely, thee shalt remember and heed this well?"

"Indeed," said the Cat, remembering his own misadventures. *"But, yet I still fail to see how this can forward our cause. Do we not want to stop the Humans?"*

"Thou art too narrow minded, Leopard, for thy own good. Lest we go over this forevermore, the Humans are too powerful. If only we compromise unto they, we shall be saved. Surely thou sees it so?"

"Still feels like running away to me," muttered the Lord of Leopards under his breath. Graechin heard him, though, and launched himself at top speed across the room, pinning the supple feline to the wall.

Claws digging in cruelly to the cat's skin and coat, he ground out, *"I know, Cat. But. We. Must. Have. PATCIENCE!!!"* He picked Polious up in his forelegs effortlessly and threw him against the wall. None moved to help the beaten Lord, not even gentle Sasoran of the Horses. Graechin glared at each of the five in turn before stomping off, leaving Polious to lick his wounds and mull over his words.

Three days passed easily for the new Bond-Mates, maybe more so than was to be expected, although neither was complaining about it. Brenna trotted back in to Jihael's forge with a smile plastered on, even though inside she was hurt. It all stemmed from the fact that *everyone* here treated her with kid's gloves, like she would shatter into a thousand thousand pieces if they didn't give her the utmost caution. Even the Elves, who obviously hated her simply for existing, would quiet down and smile their cheap, false little smiles that they always wore. Just because she was her mother's daughter, and the Dragon that currently slept inside of her.

Of course, the sealing hadn't left her unchanged: She was quicker to anger than before, and had started to speak in a roundabout way, with a hefty smattering of "Thees" and "Thines" and whatnot. Also, her movements were more lithe, and possessed a grace that was not evident there before. She sometimes felt as if she could sprout wings and fly away into the horizon. Her strength had almost doubled overnight, and didn't seem about to stop anytime soon. Her wit was quicker, and less things could dumbfound her than before.

But, it was the *principal* here! A giant She-Dragon had asked her whether she wanted to die or not. Well, what could one in her place say except yes? So, then, she was whisked away and had a bloody Dragon sealed away inside of her, one whom she had met only a few days before. She failed to see the justice in there, except that she was still alive . . . for now. "Well, at least this will even the odds, if only a little," she muttered sullenly to herself.

"What was that, love?" Jihael came out, dusting his hands together absentmindedly, a habit of his. His apron was a lighter shade of black than before, indicating a relatively new one, as they all started out white.

"Oh? Nothing, Friend Smithy. 'Twas only musings uttered aloud. My apologies," she said to him with a nod of her head.

"None needed," he answered back a mite gruffly. Apparently, everyone had trouble understanding the Dragon's and Wyrm's at first, and he was relatively new here. "C'mon, I got your things in the back." He waved her onwards, and she followed him into the small forge that was his own piece. Other blacksmiths looked out at them from behind immense anvils. More than half of them were dwarves, and half of those left were Elves. So, Jihael was in the minority here, being one of about three Half-Elves here. Immense pieces of armor, wide as Brenna was tall, loomed up out of several forges.

"What are those?" She asked curiously of the smith. He looked on them a glimmer of recognition.

"Armor, for Wyrm's and Dragon's. Most won't wear it, but a small minority of Wyrms, who got tired of being roasted alive by Dragon's, decided to pay for fire-proof armor. Costs a lot to make, and even more to pay for. Dragon's call it unsportsmanlike, and the rest of the Wyrms just turn a blind eye. Now, where the Hell did I put your new weapons?" He began to dig around in a pile of arms and armor that looked to be made for almost any fighter. After a few minutes of searching and muttering to himself, he pulled out a shiny, curved sword that looked like fluid steel. A second later, he pulled out the scabbard to it. Brenna took them both, swinging the blade around a few times. It made a swishing sound whenever she moved it, like the howl of then wind. She noticed that the scabbard had iron bands around it, up and down the sides, which meant that it could be used as a weapon or a shield in a fight.

"Pray tell, Sir Smith, how doth do such as this?" Her voice had the overawed sound of a child who had just seen their first swordfight between men.

Jihael winked at her, and smiled. "Family secret, I'd tell ya, but then I'd have to kill you." He laughed, and so did she. He went into a side room, and came back with her bow and quiver, with arrows fletched with those same peculiar arrows as her first ones (she had lost both bow and quiver sometime along the way, probably in the scramble up the mountain side). She tested its pull, and was surprised when it bent back easily. She was sweating after five pulls with her old bow, before she had had Dedira sealed away into her.

"I am glad for it, Dear Heart. I would not wish to see thee hurt," chimed in Dedira from somewhere in the vicinity of her heart.

'Ah, I had wondered whenst thou would pipe up,' she said back good-naturedly. To Jihael, she said "I thank thee, sir Jihael. Truly, thou art a master at thy art."

"Yeah, yeah," he said cheerily, waving her off. She took her cue and left with her new weapons, which she was just *aching* to test out on some hapless training area, a few dozen of which were scattered about both mountains, even if she only stayed her wanderings to Mount Dragon and those few areas of Wold that were only overlooked by the Dragons. She let Dedira ascend to the fore, and he took wing almost as soon as the white light that engulfed them, melding the two in body where they already were intertwined in soul.

He found an empty area for her to practice in, with a few upright logs to cut and targets to shoot at. He let her out, going back to wherever it was that he went in the Dreamtime. She first tested out her bow, sighting along her arrows to test their straightness. She muttered a mantra to herself, something she had picked up from a hunter a while back when she was thirteen. "Aim straight, fly far, fly true." The arrow was good; the wood was obviously from a very fine hardwood. She pulled back the bow, testing the pull again, with more feeling this time. Easily a hundred pounds, good thing she had Dedira in her now to augment her strength. The one Reytha had gotten her before (which was now lost to time and space) had had barely a forty pound pull. She placed the arrow, pulled back, and . . .

"Aim straight . . . Fly far . . . Fly TRUE!!" She let fly, and it sped down the course faster than any bird, hitting the center true from at least one hundred yards away. She heard a whistle behind her, and her sword was out in the blink of an eye, leveled at the intruder.

Herold didn't even bat an eyebrow at the offending object, just kept on grinning at her. She lowered her guard. "Pray tell, what doth thou wish?"

He smiled all the wider at her new speech patterns. "I see that the sealing worked, Naish. Now, for your form. Your left leg is too far forward, and your back is too bent."

"Eh? Who sent thee to me, and in such a cocksure and succinct manner?"

"I am here to help you train a bit, because of the all the enemies you've suddenly made here. Being a Naish isn't as neutral as was first hoped."

"What do you mean by that, neutral? Pray tell, as I am left in the dark on this matter."

"Well, the Naish were created as a sort of peace core between the Dragons and Wyrms and the rest. Humans and Elves would make a pact with an animal whom they had come to call friend, and they would become Bonded by the Seal. Since the common side to them could find common ground, most wars between the two could, hopefully, be avoided. Sadly, they took sides in the conflicts as well, so that idea went to Hell."

"So, pray tell, if such a broken accoutrement were to be within our midst's, why keep it as such? Should it not have been abandoned long ago? And, pray, why are there not Dwarves added unto this pact?"

"I see that having Dedira sealed into you has expanded your vocabulary, Brenna. As to the first question, we continue it because it is tradition. A tradition, if I recall correctly, saved your life. As to the second, well . . . it is in the entire mindset of the Dwarf folk. They are very jealous of their bodies, and cringe with the thought of sharing it with anyone, which is also why they show no mercy to the possessed when they find them. Now, to the bloody lesson!" He cut her off when she had once again opened her mouth. He drew his blade out. "This is Lilith, the Biter. Have you named your blade yet?"

"Why would I do as such."

Dedira answered for the frustrated Half-Elf before them. *"Giving them a name gives them life, it gives them personality, and, as such, it gives them power, more so than any unnamed blade."*

"Oh . . . I see," she said aloud, to answer both of her companions. "But, I don't know any real Elvish. Can I . . . get a little help?" She pulled the dreaded puppy-eyes on him, even going so far as to make a few tears well up for added effect.

"Alright, alright," he said, laughing. "Bloody dramatist," he added under his breath. "Let me take a closer look at it."

She handed it over, and he marveled at it, testing it out with a few swings. It made a sound like the wind before the storm, howling in a low voice that was welcome to the ears. He ran his hand along the length, and smiled at its strength, and how true the blade was. He gripped the hilt fully now, and marveled how it would respond seamlessly to his every whim, almost as if he could think only and it would do it. He reverently handed it back to her. "I would say *Jahlsakend*, The Wind Blade. Truly, it will live up to it."

She ran her hand down the blade reverently, before she heard his sword unsheathing. He got into a battle stance, smirking a little bit. "Right, lets see the damage. Have at you!" She barely had time to bring her sword up to block, and even then it was pushed aside, Lilith whistling past her ear and clipping off a bit of her hair. She gaped open mouthed at him. "Always keep your guard up, and don't stare like that, makes you look stupid."

She forcibly slammed her jaw shut. "Wait, shouldn't we find someway to keep ourselves from being slashed into bloody shreds?"

"Well, if you want. Give her here," he said, motioning to Brenna's blade. She gave it to him, mystified. He ran his hand over the blade, and muttered "Hurn-sul." Where his hand had just been, a glow encompassed the newly christened Jahlsakend, and quickly dispersed into the blade. He handed it back to her, and did the same to Lilith. He placed his hand on the edge and went through the motions of cutting himself. Nothing happened. "Low level Sealing spell, contains the edge of any weapon. Perfect for practice. Now, shall we?" He got back into his stance, and she got into her sad little imitation of one. He sighed heavily. "No, no, no! Put your front leg back more, and bring your back leg a little more to the fore, it'll make you a bit faster on the receiving end of a strike, and vice-versa. Also, your left arm is too low, bring it just a smidge higher."

She made the necessary improvements, and was almost able to block his next strike.

Almost. Something told her that this would be a long, hard, and *painful* day.

Brenna dragged her sore, sorry carcass back to the temporary place she'd be calling a room. Herold had shown her everything, it seemed, the hard way. But, on the pseudo-bright side, she now knew that she was nigh on a hopeless case when it came to swordsmanship, but excelled at archery. Too bad that Naish were swordsman.

"Tis a tradition," explained Dedira patiently. Unfortunately, she was in no mood for patience. She fell onto the bed, chest heaving, throat burning.

"Go bugger off, damn you," she stated flatly, too tired to think it back to him.

"Alas for thee, Love, tis not my fault that thou art such a short case in the arts of war."

'That as it may be, you still are an annoying, babyish overgrown lizard with wings. So you can just shut up now, please and thank you.'

"Why, I am hurt!" His voice held a slight mocking edge.

'Why you little-'

"Brenna?" Reytha stood in the doorway, a concerned look on her face. "You alright?"

Brenna managed a smile from where she lay on the bed, tilting her neck up just enough to see her friend. "Oh, yeah. Except I feel as if I have gone through seven of the nine Hells. Pray tell, what is the matter?"

Reytha laughed lightly at her. "I see that Dedira is rubbing off on you. You want a drink?"

"Much 'preciated," she muffled into her pillow, which had somehow gotten over her face. The Kitsune vanished in a flare of fox-fire, returning a few moments later with a cold glass of water. Brenna was too tired to wonder why the water wasn't boiling after contact with the fox-fire, which could melt steel in a few moments. She merely guzzled down the cool liquid. Nodding her thanks, she waited for her friend to speak.

"Well, you feeling better, Dear-Heart?" Another nod. "Good. I am here to help you in your magic, which is currently nonexistent."

Brenna paled a little, but couldn't muster the energy to really care. "Uh, Reytha?"

"Yes?"

"Goodnight." Brenna blew out the candle next to her bed, leaving her friend in the dark. Reytha chuckled a bit.

"Sleep well . . . kit." Eight tails waving behind her serenely, she left down the hallway.

9

He gazed, helplessly, as he watched them cut his friends down. A howl split the night air, tearing into his soul. He knew that cry, of pain, of loss. He cringed, hoping that his eyes had betrayed him.

Blood . . . so much that he felt as if he would drown in it forever. He knew that there was something he could do, should do . . . but was too afraid. Their enemies surrounded them, cackling in glee.

The snake came out of its hiding place, hissing menacingly at him. He tried to move as it bore down on him, but his legs were frozen in terror. He was hopeless in his helplessness. He wanted to cry, to let the world pass him by and be done with it.

The snake came closer, and he heard another scream. Newer . . . still fresh in his memories . . . the cry of a girl who he had sworn to protect. "NO!!!!!" It seemed that only his voice could work now, as it did no good except to draw attention to himself. He only screamed at them louder.

They smiled their cruel, evil, misguided smiles. "We have succeeded . . ." Their voices held a ghostly, ethereal feel to them . . . the voice of the Damned.

"She is ours now, she is ours now, she is ours now . . ." They began their mocking chant, a mantra of lust and loss and pure dark. "She is ours now, she is our now, she is—"

"SHE IS MINE!" They quieted, cowed by the specter. **"BOTH ARE, NOW. STAND ASIDE, FOOLS!"** They, the nameless, faceless foe, moved as tide before the beach, flowing fluidly into the rocks of whence they came. Darkness and shadows consumed them. All had left . . . but a flash, a flame that contested this great blackness. Fire mixed with blood as his friend stood before the Great Dark.

"Go . . . go back. It is not yet her time. Not . . . yet . . . !"

"FOOL, YOU KNOW NOT YOUR PLACE. NONE CONTEST MY WILL!" The Darkness paid her no heed, and moved closer to the fallen one. Bodies of the dead and dying were consumed in Its all reaching Shadow.

"A . . . an exchange . . . my life . . . for hers."

"BUT SOFT, THY WILL AND COURAGE AMUSE ME. TELL ME, FOX WHELP, WHY DO YOU THROW YOURSELF TO ME FOR THIS . . . DAMNED ONE. SHE IS DOOMED UNTO ME IN NOT LONG. WHY GIVE THYSELF FOR HER, WHEN SHE WILL DIE SO SOON ANYWAY?"

"All Prophecy will not come true . . . I believe that . . . that she can . . . change her destiny—"

"NONE CAN CHANGE FATE!!!"

"Not even you?"

"NOR I . . . NOR THEE, FOOL. I AM THE OMNIPOTENT, I AM THE SPECTER OF DOOM AND SARK"

"Sing your praises, if you must . . . but, I will not stand by and let her fall . . . not now, not . . . EVER!" More blood flowed from her torn side.

"WHY DOTH THOU GIVE THY LIFE FOR THIS ONE? SURELY, YOU FIND THYSELF MORE VALUABLE?"

"Because . . . she is precious to me . . . and I swore to protect her."

"SHE IS NOT THY KIT," said the specter, mimicking the words spoken to her not so long ago.

"But I will give my life for her, all the same." Her voice held conviction, something that had been all but gone until then.

"EVEN THE LIKES OF I CANNOT CONTEST THE WILL OF AGES. LEST I DOOM THEE ALL . . . DEPART FROM HERE, LIVE WELL, AND FORGET OF THIS."

"I cannot. I . . . will NOT forsake her."

"IT IS DESTINY."

"You said . . . that Fate demands a death here?"

"IT IS DESTINY THAT SHE DIE." His voice brooked no argument.

"But that . . . that she does not have to die now?"

"IT IS FATE . . . THAT SOMEONE HERE DIES," He admitted solemnly.

"Then . . . why can't I . . . replace her? Is not one soul . . . as good as another?"

"FATE CRIES FOR TWO."

"Then . . . take me as well." Voice found, he let out a shaky breath. "Take my life for hers, take her life for his." The girl in question had a hole in her chest . . . it went straight through her heart, the only place which could wound them both. She had suffered so much . . . Could he stand to take away her newfound brother?

The Specter grabbed the insignificant Flame, snuffing it out almost contemptuously. He moved to Daima. He looked into his eyes.

Nine fiery red tails fell to the ground softly in death, as Daima Udun looked into the eyes of Death.

He screamed, and he felt a soul ripped from him.

"Daima? DAIMA!!!! WAKE UP!!!!" He shot up in a cold sweat, water soaking through the bed sheets he lay fitfully on. He looked around in surprise; he had been in the Dreamscape, last he remembered.

"What . . . what happened?" He asked it aloud, for fear of not being able to think it back correctly.

"You had another vision. The Sight is true upon you . . . I let you out, so as to stop it before you damaged yourself. A scar of the mind can be even more damaging than one of the body." Daima couldn't help but smile as his friend mimicked the words of their old instructor, Sashim.

Controlling his racing heart a little, he managed to calm down a bit. *'Thanks.'*

"No problem. Do you remember what you saw?" Daima gasped, as those eyes . . .

He started to weep, unable to control himself. *"What did you see?"*

He beat upon the bed in anger, still shedding tears at his impunity, his helplessness. *"What did you see?"*

Daima Udun, who had unflinchingly faced down enemies that most would hardly find in their worst nightmares, gave a heart wrenching sob of sheer despair. *"WHAT DID YOU SEE, DAMN YOU!!!??!?!"*

"I SAW DEATH!!!!" He started to quietly sob to himself as Nainya only looked on in fear. Death would come . . . soon.

For Brenna. So that Prophecy was fulfilled.

For what seemed the twelfth dozen time that week alone, she collapsed onto the loamy ground. Reytha sighed, and shook her head in sympathy and a little amusement. What Brenna lacked in skill and power she made up for in determination and a quick mind. She had only mastered around six simple spells, and those barely at that. She helped Brenna up, grunting with the effort. Brenna gazed at her a little drowsily, then shook her head to clear it. "Thanks."

"Not a problem. Now, lets see what happened wrong, hmm? So, you did the correct seals and all, but still managed to drain most of your energy away, correct? Well, my guess'd be that you simply let your internal shields down."

"Sorry, what? I can't think straight at the moment."

"Right . . . well, each person has two types of shields, Internal and External. This ring a bell?" The girl shook her head, no. "Right, so they each protect from magical attacks and energies. Anything?"

"Slightly . . . except I never really learned it all that well. May as well explain it over again."

Reytha sighed, all eight tails twitching a little in irritation. "Alright then . . . Magical attacks are universal and unshifting. Magic is Magic, no matter what. If Magic is used with the intent to kill, then it *will* kill someone. If you use an attack that affects a large area with you in it, than you are as likely to suffer its effects as your enemies. That's where Internal shields come in. They protect you from *your* magic, whereas External shields will deflect an enemies attacks. Making any sense now?"

"Nope. But can I just nod my head and we go on to find some way to make me better at it?"

Reytha sighed heavily. "Honestly, Dear-Heart, I don't know whether you're a pip or a git."

"Or both."

"Yes, or both. Lets try yet again, shall we?"

With a groan, Brenna began the seals and words for the spell.

"Lest we tarry ere long, let us begin. Our designs, so carefully laid out, may prove ineffective, as of now. Alas, she is but true! Prophecy will be fulfilled!"

"Oh, don't be so worried. Naught is set in stone, least of all Prophecy. It will only come true if you make it."

Graechin stiffened, then brought one immense eye up to the half-elf, looking her in both of her eyes. **"Pray tell, mortal, what didst thou say? Lest mine ears and eyes both deceive me, you said that 'I' would insinuate this foul ledger. Did I hear true, dear-heart?"** Contrary to his words, there was no hint of affection in the honorific.

She did not stir, nay, nor even show any fear at all! "What you heard was true. But," she added when the Lord of Wyrms reared up in anger, "I meant that Prophecy will be fulfilled only if you let it. Kill her, and it shall be done with, once and for all."

"Alas, tis not as easy as first thought. She has powerful allies, and has been imbued with one of the thrice cursed House Dragon."

Her eyes widened in surprise, but only a little. She knew that such might have happened, in the end. "She is a Naish now?"

"Aye, that she is. She is well protected, indeed. And getting stronger by the day. Your month is nigh on ended, and I fear that my subordinates may not be able to dispatch her in a timely manner before then."

"Then let me."

"But soft, Halfling, you must jest! Surely, thou could not dispatch as such as the Demon Ledger so easily, nor upon the Mount of the Dragons!"

"No. I don't say I can, and I am not fool enough to risk it. Send her away . . . to High Point, at least. There, me and my people will send her to an early grave. Fear not, as I shall attend to it personally."

"Good, good. But . . . how shall I send her away? Lest ye hath forgotten, she is protected by the might of Dragon, and they are not easily fooled, curse them! Surely, I cannot send her to this place, alone, unguarded, without suspicion?"

"Make a mission of it. Send her and a few others on a mission to assassinate the Emperor of all Humans. Surely, they'd listen to that?"

The giant Wyrm contemplated it a moment. *"Aye . . . that they would. I thank thee for thy kindness and wit in such matters. I see that thou art truly a master of thy art!"*

Eileen smiled like a fox. "What can I say? Subterfuge is in my blood."

"That it is. That it is." She started out the immense passage, which led to her ride, a different Wyrm named Tryul. Fools all.

'It is all for you, Mistress. I shall make you proud.'

"That you will, Daughter. That you will."

Once again, she got into her stance, bringing the wispy blade to bear. Herold looked on approvingly, before moving into his own stance, similar to hers. Except, his was made to more openly accommodate the added thickness of his own sword, which easily doubled, even tripled Brenna's in weight. "Ready?" She nodded wearily, wondering whether or not this wad her twelfth or thirteenth spar in the last two or so hours. Herold had beaten her each time . . . miserably too. "Then . . . *ulin!*" Even as he shouted the word to begin their match, he was springing towards her at an unbelievable speed. She barely had time to block his strike, and even then he broke through her guard. She jumped back hastily, bringing her blade back up.

She ducked under his next attack, making a blind strike that missed widely. He used his next effort in a series of precise strikes that would have been deadly had the blades not been dulled. She only barely managed to block them, her movements clumsy despite her blade. His, at the same time, were fluid and natural, as if he were born into the fight. She struck out, but in desperation this time. He blocked it offhandedly, then came at her again. The worst part: She could tell he only used a fraction of his true skill. *'This isn't working!'* She ducked under another swing, only to catch the backhand of it, sending her sprawling unceremoniously. She groaned, breathing out rather huffily.

"Lets call it a day, shall we? I think you are doing better."

'Pfft, yeah, and I'm also about to sprout wings and a long nose and become a hummingbird.'

"If this style of swordplay works not for thee," chimed in Dedira, *"then why not use a different one? Something more suited to thy blade?"*

'First bright idea I've heard all day.' She stood up. "Wait."

Herold paused, looking at her. "Yes?"

"Pray, give me but . . . a few minutes to gather back my wind, and then . . . a rematch?"

He grinned. "Why not?"

She smiled at him, then gratefully sat on the ground. She closed her eyes, making it look like she was meditating. In all actuality, she was conversing heatedly with Dedira. *'Right . . . so, I need a style that would let me use speed as well as strength, which I now have thanks to you. Any ideas?'*

"But a one. What of . . . this?" Several images flashed through her minds eye, outlining a new stance and set of strikes. She even saw a few kicks and punches in there. She went through it twice more, before she thought that she got it down.

'Thanks.'

"No need, Dear-Heart. Tis but my humble pleasure."

'Damn Overgrown Lizard,' she said affectionately. She and Dedira had only been bonded maybe a week or so, and already she looked on him as an older brother. A large, scaly, fire-spewing older brother. She bit her lip, slightly nervous, but then stood back up, being careful so as to not show any fear or hesitation. "Ready?"

Herold shook his head in amusement. "That's my line," he muttered. He got into his tried and true stance, and Brenna to hers. He was surprised to see her in an entirely different one than him, not even resembling his teachings. Her legs, for one thing, were spaced closer together, and her blade was held on an angle, almost next to her eye; as opposed to his, which was held in front to make slashing easier. Hers looked more on par to a thrusting blade stance. "What the . . . ? Ulin!" He charged right at her. When he swung at a downwards angle, she sidestepped; and, *incredibly*, struck him on the side. He winced as he felt the bruise sure to form there. She had given her all to that swing: if she hadn't just wasted most of her energies on the sparring beforehand she would probably have broken a few of his ribs. "What the . . . ?"

"My new style, Dedira came up with most of it though. It's obvious that your style is better suited to men like you: strong, powerful, but a mite on the slow side. My style uses speed *and* strength, which I now have in spades." Herold could only whistle in astonishment (and, yes, in *pride*) from his seat on the dusty earth of the training ground they were now frequenting. She offered a hand to help him up, which he took.

"And you two came up with that in just under a few minutes?"

"Yep," she answered brightly, despite her obvious fatigue.

"Brenna, you never cease to amaze me." He smiled congenially at her. "And," he added under his breath in a whisper, "you prove more and more that you are Prophecy."

"What was that?" She had yet to master her heightened senses, so she missed a lot of what was said. Extra sensitive hearing (for her, at least), took a bit of getting used to.

"Huh?" He had forgotten that Dedira was her Bond-Brother, and Dragons have the best sense of hearing anyway. "Oh, nothing!"

Abruptly, she yawned, fatigue catching up to her. "Well, I think I'll turn in for a good nap. Excuse me, I wouldn't trust my legs to carry me so far. There are some perks to being Naish, I see." She yawned again, mightier than before. Then, she was consumed in a soft incandescence as she let Dedira come out. The Dragon didn't look at all happy, to say the least.

"Mayhaps Brenna has yet to master herself yet, but I have." He, ever so much, stretched the 'I' in that sentence. **"Doth thou speak of what I fear?"**

"Can she hear us?" Worry leaked into his voice.

"Nay, she is but asleep now. Thy teachings are . . . effective, to say but the least."

Herold sighed in relief. "Good. Some things she is best off not knowing."

"Agreed. Much as it pains me so . . . she is not ready for such a burden. Am I correct to assume that she is to unite the Clans . . . at the cost of herself?"

Herold nodded his head in reply. "Aye. Unless something big happens real soon . . . I just hope that we're proved wrong." He turned to leave, but not before bowing to the Dragon.

"Me as well . . . my friend . . ." He took to wing, letting the gentle air currents guide him, instinct showing him which to travel to get to the place where he and Brenna called home. *'Sleep well, Sister . . . sleep well,'* he thought wistfully.

"Overgrown Lizard . . . lemme sleep, damnit," she replied sleepily. He could only chuckle slightly at that. Cries split the night air, reminders

of the dangers they now faced. He only hoped that they were the only things.

Some things are far worse than death. Far worse.

"ANOTHER ROUND!!!!" Daima smashed his now much abused mug in front of the now very much peeved dwarfs nose. He had downed some two or so *dozen* mugs worth of strong ale. He was, thankfully, one of those "Happy" drunks. He was *beyond* plastered, if possible. But, then, Daima had always been one to push limits, whether it was his liver's endurance or the said peeved dwarfs' patience, which both were wearing thin. "Waiter, 'nother round, damnit!"

In as calm a voice as he could, the dwarf ground out, "*Sir*, I believe that you have had enough ale. Would you. PLEASE! Leave. Now. Thank you."

Drunk or no, Daima never knew when to take a hint. Even one this obvious. "Nonshense! I'm not swear, I drunk! I mean, I'm drunk swear, I not! Err . . . WAITER!!! 'nother round, if ye would, thanshk," he slurred. It was true, Daima had found a new level of drunkenness.

"You should get a medal. Now, could you please stop?"

"Whasshamatta, Nainya? Lose yer stomack fer drinkin'? Whassha lil' ale 'twixt friends?" He was too drunk to think anything even close to coherent, as he was in that happy little place between happy hour and hangovers. Truly, bliss.

"Please leave, *SIR*, before I get my axe." Under his breath, the dwarf muttered, "I hate my job."

"Daima?" Reytha poked her head into the normally bustling room, now home to only two inhabitants. She stepped inside, nose crinkling at the smell of alcohol. She gagged a little, but still pushed onwards to her friend. "Daima, why are you still here?"

"I'm happy . . . is you happy?"

"Am I going to have to pay for this little habit of yours . . . again?" He only laughed (a bit on the hysterical side). "I'll take that as a yes. Come on, time to go home."

He wasn't listening to her, being enraptured by her swaying tails. "Ooooh . . . pretty. Can I play?" Reytha shook her head and side, not sure whether to be amused or simply pity the poor soul. "'Nother round?" His voice held a whining quality that she heard when kits wanted to stay out and play a little more.

"Nope, sorry. No "nother round'."

"She's right, you know," chimed in Nainya.

He shook his head, as if to clear it. It was a sad, futile attempt. "Damn fluffball wants me ta stop . . . but I am better than him," he muttered. Then, shouting out to the world in a scream (the "whole world", at the moment, consisted of Reytha, the bartender, and whoever was within the vicinity of . . . around six miles), "'cause I HAVE OPPOSABLE THUMBS!!!!!" He wiggled said appendages in front of the now peeved Kitsunes nose. He giggled like a little girl . . . which creeped out both of said occupants.

"Ooh, I'm so hurt. This coming from the drunkard who can't hold his ale after three mugs worth."

"Shaddup, least I can standup on two legs . . ."

"Are you talking to Nainya?" Her tails twitched irritatedly.

"Yeppers, that damn wolf what lives in my head . . . he's just jealous 'cause I gots thumbs."

"That may be so, but I think that you should let him walk now."

"Naw, I'm jus' fine on me own." At this point, he got up from the bar stool he had been sitting on, and promptly tripped on one of those troublesome pieces of dust that so carelessly littered the floor. The only thing that saved him from breaking his nose was the arrival of Reytha's eight tails, which easily supported his weight. Once again enraptured by the red, fiery tails, he began to pet them.

Reytha blushed, and promptly let him fall to the ground via slipping her tails away. Prehensile tails have their uses. Also, one is best not to pet them when a Kitsune is in their human form, as they are . . . well, rather *sensitive* to the touch near the base, which was where Daima had been petting.

Nainya inwardly winced from the place in his Dreamscape where he resided. *"Ouch. And worst is, I haven't even gotten drunk. Curse complete sealing . . . oi, luku-ne, time to wake up. Or, just let me out, and you can avoid one very, VERY bad hangover."*

"Don' care . . . pain means I can't feel nothin' but it. Pains good. Let me feel it . . . s'all I gots left." He saw her tails again, and reached for them like a child would. "Pretty . . ."

She got tired of this, and shook him roughly by the shoulders, seeming to clear his head for a bit. "Reytha? That . . . that you?"

"Yes. Now, lets get gone, before you manage to make an even bigger fool of yourself, although I'm not sure how that's possible." She trailed off when she noticed that he had started sobbing. "What's wrong? Don't tell me that you're crying over the fact you can't drink anymore today."

Instead, she got almost a coherent answer. "Oh, it was . . . it wuz jus' so 'orrible! Those eyes . . . those eyes!!! They was . . . I looked into 'em, and then they was the ones what looked into me!" He sobbed brokenly into her shoulder.

'The darker side of heroes,' she thought grimly of it. "What? What did you see? Who's eyes?"

"Don't wanna talk none 'bout it," he said darkly.

"Stop being so damnedly stubborn! I can't help if you won't let me in! Back off," she warned the dwarf, who had stopped pretending to polish the mugs left behind in favor of eavesdropping. He moved off sullenly; as he had been enjoying Daima make an ass of himself.

"You can't help . . . who gots nine?"

"Wha'?" She honestly had no clue as to what he was going on about

"Which a you damn foxes gots nine tails?" His voice was more sober now, almost as if the past three dozen mugs hadn't been. Ah, if only it were true. At that point, Daima's stomach decided that ale wasn't to its liking, and expelled it back from whence it came. He threw up onto the stone floor, narrowly missing the eight-tails bare feet.

"C'mon . . . time for bed." She cast a small spell that would lessen the effects of the booze (interestingly, no spell has ever been found to completely get rid of a hangover, making it truly a universal ill). Using her tails gingerly, she picked up the now snoring man, leaving a few coins on the counter. They could put the rest on his tab, which already was of almost mythic proportions.

For now, she would simply let it lie. She had a headache.

He sniffed the air once again. Yes, there it was. Wyrm stench. He could not mistake that foul odor for anything else. Cautiously, Dedira gained a little height, so that he surfed level on to the clouds. Yes, there they were; right in front of where Brenna's small room. He counted two, no, *three* Wyrms there, all bigger than he by a few heads. He did not like the odds at all. He had no need to wonder as to why they were patronizing his home, as the girl bound to his heart and mind forevermore was reason enough. He wheeled about over them, seeing if they were there to attack or simply keep him out. Both, it seemed, as one of them launched up after him while the others stayed put, almost stubbornly.

It took less than a minute for the Wyrm to reach hailing distance. **"Pray tell, sirrah, why do you not allow one access unto his own hold?"** The Wyrm did not miss the insult that unconsciously found voice in the Dragon.

"Tis naught of thy concern, O Naish," he said with equal venom. **"We are but dawdling a while. Surely, you would not contest us a slight respite from our long journey?"**

"Unto where didst thou journey? And why doth thou and thy companions seek refuge in a Dragon's hold? Surely one more . . . suitable . . . unto thy needs is available nearby?"

The Wyrm did not miss the hidden threat. His jaw began to twitch slightly, showing his sharp teeth and fangs. "Tis not thy concern, Dragon."

"Who sent you?" No answer from the slowly wheeling Wyrm. "Who sent you?"

"None. We went alone unto a Human settlement and laid waste to it."

"Then not only doth thou trespass, thou art a fool! We await the arrival of our allies, and thy play could cost us much, much more!"

"TIS NOT THY CONCERN!!!!" The Wyrm had finally lost his temper, making a clumsy lunge at Dedira. The Dragon nimbly danced around the teeth and claws, beating back slightly. He did not wish to spill blood here, now.

Another Wyrm flew up, leaving only one to guard his hold. "What of it? Harirh, let it be; this one is not worth the time to slay."

"HAH! I cannot away, for this one has left a stain upon my honor," shot back the first Wyrm, Harirh.

"Thou would have to possess such a thing first for it to be stained," Dedira said in a barbed way. Both Wyrms hissed at him in anger, but Harirh had seemed to calm a bit after his verbal reprimand. "Away from my hold, as I am tired and do not wish to fight. If thou must, then come back ere the morrows eve. I shall await, fresh and ready. If thou would?" He motioned to the Wyrm at his doorway.

The second Wyrm, obviously the leader, roared out at the one still on the ground, who promptly flew up to level. They glared heatedly at the Dragon before leaving for the Mount Wyrm. Dedira flew down to his and Brenna's hold, which was halfway up Mount Dragon. He sighed heavily as he landed, and managed to squeeze through the smallish doorway. He lay down, resting his head on his forefeet, feeling the adrenaline of the almost-battle wearing away.

'Brenna? Art thou awake yet?"

". . . Stupid Fox, let me have the salmon, greedy sunova . . ." He shook his head in amusement. Even in the Dreamscape, Brenna mumbled in her sleep. He let his eyes close, intent on sleeping for a few hours now. He would need it, now more than ever.

He only hoped that it, whatever it would be, happened soon.

10

"Oooooh . . . my head. What happened?"

"You got piss drunk, said you were better than me because you had opposable thumbs, and nearly threw up on Reytha. Overall, a rather productive night, no?"

"Oh . . . oh," was all he could say. He rubbed his throbbing temples, and sighed heavily. He looked around the room he was in, conspicuously not his at all. For one thing, it had too much pink in it. "Where am I?"

"Reytha's room. She couldn't remember where yours was, so she just dumped you here."

'Where is she, then?' He had finally managed to start thinking again through the skull splitting pain that happened after he got smashed in the real world. "That's why I prefer to drink with the dwarves in my head," he muttered under his breath.

"Well, Reytha turned into her fox form and slept on the floor, and the dwarves are probably singing a drinking song right now. I bet they miss you so."

'Screw off, dumb ass, I'm in no mood right now.'

"Awww, wittle biddy baby sad 'cause he don't have his bottle?"

'Ooooh . . . why did I agree to get Bonded to you again?'

"Because you were young and stupid. Now, you're older and still stupid. Good for you."

"Shut it, fluffball," he said aloud.

"I was sleeping, thank you very much," said Reytha from her place on the floor. It was odd to see a fox speaking his language, but Daima had gotten used to it after a while. She stood, stretched, then changed into her human form. She gave him a 'Well-I-am-waiting-so-you-better-make-this-excuse-good' look, one he knew all too well.

94

"I was talking to Nainya. Love the guy, but he can get real annoying sometimes."

"That's what you get for having a wolf inside your skull. Now, want to tell me why you went on a binge last night?"

"Uh . . . drowning out premonitions?" He offered.

"Yeah, right. Mind giving me the truth?"

"Not the most," he muttered. Then, louder, "I guess it's . . . a little more complicated than I expected."

"Is it the Sight?"

He gaped at her openmouthed. "You *knew*?"

"Well, it's kind of obvious. People with the Sight give off a distinctive smell, and you're not as clever as you think." She looked smug, and probably was, when it came right down to it.

He gulped. "How many more know?"

"Probably all of the Kitsunes, a few wolves, the Dragons, and whoever else they decided to tell."

He hung his head in defeat. "Oh, I am so *screwed*. So very screwed. I am screwed," he repeated to himself. After the fifth verse of this particular poem, Reytha shook him gently by the shoulders.

"That isn't important right now. What's done is done. Now, the important thing is, what did you see?" She looked him in the eyes.

He gulped again, mouth going dry. "I don't know. There was . . . Death. Lots of it. And Brenna and me and half-Elves and a Kitsune and I DON'T KNOW!!!!" He had started in almost a whisper, but had ended in a mighty shout. Reytha didn't flinch. He shook his head, as if to clear it. "Sorry. I don't know what I saw, exactly, but I know that it isn't good at all. If you'll excuse me, I need a walk." He grabbed his cloak off the stand where it had fallen the night before, shrugging it on quickly. Taking long strides, he took off. She let him go.

He needed it.

"Ulin!" Herold shouted before he charged at her. She deftly sidestepped his thrust, blade trying to catch him while he was facing from her. He twisted around in what looked like an uncomfortable way, and blocked her blow. "Good, Brenna. You're getting better at it. Soon you'll need a new teacher, one better than me."

She looked at him in confusion. "There are people that much better than you?"

He smiled ruefully. "Don't act surprised; there's always someone better. But, still, I think that you are ready for a new teacher. You are easily surpassing me, what with your new style, and I think it would be better if you found a new teacher, who has more experience with a style like yours."

"Who? In case you don't remember, I am kinda new here."

He held up his hands, as if to placate her. "I know, and that's why I'll help you out here. No worries, right?"

She smiled. "Nope." She sheathed her sword in its scabbard. "If you don't think that I can benefit from this anymore today, do you mind if I take a break? There are some things that I need to mull over. Alone."

"Yeah . . . sure. See you around?"

"Why not? I haven't got anything better to do," she joked. She smiled brightly, and turned to leave. As she walked away, Herold watched her. He sighed.

"Truly, Brenna'Adun'Kial, you are a sign. Gevorh protect, for I doubt that I can." He sheathed his own blade, and walked away, not looking back.

"Running away won't solve anything," said Nainya again for what seemed the fifth time that minute. He had only been walking for a quarter hour now, hardly out of the tunnels yet. He sighed heavily at his best friend.

'Maybe, but I think I know what I'm doing. Could you let me be? Last time I checked, I already had a conscience.'

"But I'm so much better at it," said the wolf in mock hurt.

'Nainya, listen . . . could you, maybe . . . leave me alone? Just for a little while, I . . . I need to be alone for now." There was such seriousness in his voice that Nainya did not joke about it all.

He simply said, *"Okay,"* and Daima felt him leave for his Dreamscape.

Daima smiled. "Good." He continued walking, eyes downcast as he was lost inside his own thoughts. Could his Sight really be so attuned to the future so quickly? Usually, it took several years before one could see images like he had, and he had only started getting the signs a couple of weeks ago. Could it have to do with Brenna? Maybe, but he wasn't so sure. Maybe they were simple nightmares . . . but he was not one to remember nightmares, even ones so vivid.

So intent was he on his musings that he failed to notice the girl to whom his thoughts were turning. She was lost in thought too (actually, a conversation with Dedira). So, neither noticed the other coming until they collided mid-hallway.

Brenna fell back, managing to throw her hands back so they caught the fall. Daima fell on his ass. He grimaced, and then helped her up. "Sorry," he muttered in an embarrassed way.

"S'alright," she muttered right back. He rubbed the back of his head, trying to think of something witty to shatter the awkward moment. While he waited for his sluggish mind to catch up to his mouth, he took in her new look. No longer in the threadbare homespun she had worn when he first met her, she was now clothed in a rich woolen shirt and leggings, a cloak hanging loosely from her shoulders. All of it was a deep blue that blended with the mountain wall. Her black hair had grown a little now, reaching beyond her shoulders. Her skin, while still unnaturally pale, held a tanned quality now that made her look better in this light. He almost missed what she said next, so intent was he on thinking of something to say.

"Daima, why do you all fight the Humans here? I never really got that part . . . history was never my forte."

Daima grimaced. "Well, it all started, I guess, a few years back, maybe a decade or so ago. You see, a great Sorceress, Mab, had come down out of the Mountains of Dangand. She was powerful in the Shadow Arts, where she cast her will upon the weak minded. She quickly gained control of all the trolls, ogres, and whatnot that live beyond the border. She was one of the few humans able to do magic, but it was at the cost of her sanity. This was her third Coming. She believed that the Lands of Gevorh's Pride belonged solely to her, and declared war on all four nations with her large army. It had, at the least, some hundred thousands of beasts and monsters. I'd tell you how she was defeated, but that would take all day, and Reytha remembers it better than me anyway. Anyway, when she was defeated, there returned the uneasy alliance betwixt the Humans, Elves, Dwarves, and the Wold. I was a friend of the King, Troshien. He went mad for power, and declared that magic was an abomination. Of course, he couldn't use it."

"If we had magic and they didn't, shouldn't it have been an easy victory? I mean, even I know that magic isn't omnipotent, but it can do some real damage in the right hands."

"You normally would be correct, but for two things. The first is that there are far more humans than Elves and Dwarves combined, even without the Hunter tribes. The Empire sought to duplicate magics through the use of science. They couldn't, but still came pretty damn close, and are growing more sophisticated by the year. Soon, we shant even have magic's advantage. After *he* declared us all abominations and debasements to science, he took it upon himself to eradicate us all. So started the great Hunt, where all known Elven and Dwarven cities and villages that were known by Troshien were destroyed. The survivors were hunted down and exterminated. Thousands died on both sides. It was chaos incarnate. The Elves retreated into their forest holds, and the Dwarves into the Harahd Mountains. The Dragons continued raiding human settlements, although it's getting harder. After that, we consolidated our forces, not meeting their armies in force. Our will was shattered, and many thought of fleeing across the sea. But we don't."

"Why not? If it is so hopeless, then why do you continue to fight for it? Is it not a lost cause?" Her voice held an accusing trait in it, and he sighed heavily.

"It is not for ourselves that we fight. It is the Wonder. The humans . . . their scientists, they seek to catalog and categorize *everything* in the world. They want . . . to find out everything there is to know. They want to destroy the Wonder that's left in this world, the magical things that we don't know the why about, just that they are and, if we can help it, always will be."

She regarded him thoughtfully for a moment. Then, "You should be a bard. You've got the drama needed for it."

He nearly fell to the floor in disbelief. "I was being serious here!"

She smiled innocently. "So was I."

Horns sounded in the deep. "They're here," said Daima reverently.

"Who? Who's here?"

"Yoreh and his Elves. The wheels are finally beginning to turn. Thank Gevorh." He turned and grabbed her hand abruptly, dragging her back along from whence she had come. To the light.

Brenna's eyes widened at the sight. Before her was an army. Not just a fighting force, but an *Army*. A big one. Rows upon rows of Elves in shining armor, glinting gold in the sunlight that dazzled her weary eyes, gleaming gold in the sunlight of the early morning. She could only watch, dazed, as rows upon rows upon shining rows marched ever closer.

Thousands of Elves, making the hills and the very mountains, it seemed, to tremble with every step of the immense juggernaut. At least twenty thousand Elves marched to Wold, greeted by cheers by all of the people there already. Some with bows, others with swords or pikes, and some with all three. A few rode upon the backs of strange, horse-like creatures, who seemed stronger, faster, and downright meaner than their gentler counterparts. Their eyes were slitted, giving them a fierce reptilian visage. The sleek sheen of their coats cast a glimmer about them that rendered them with a fierce and terrible beauty. Their hooves, if one would venture to call them so, were shaped into three different spikes that flattened when they reached the ground. A perfect battle steed. Before this great host rode the Elven Royalty, some dozen or so princes, retainers, guards, and the King and Queen.

But that was not all. Behind the Elven host came an army of Dwarves, fifteen thousand strong, carrying their preferred axes, hammers, ands mallets. They were half as tall as a man (whereas some of the Elves were half as tall again). They were adorned in uniform armor, and the only unique thing to them, it seemed, was their helmets. Each was adorned as the Dwarf saw fit, whether it be with markings, horns, nose guards, or simply battle scars from the war with the goblins a few years ago. Before them strode casually their Lords, who would be damned before mounting any steed.

Both armies came to a halt at the same time. Standards fluttered in the breeze, whipping and snapping as if fit to break free. No one spoke.

Then, out came Fafnir, Graechin, Brithal, and Kaiden of the Griffins. They towered above all of the Elves, although they seemed not to care much for that. Fafnir bowed low, and Brithal and Kaiden mimicked her. Graechin bowed shallowly, showing his true arrogance. They started to speak, and though Brenna could not hear it, she could tell that it was quickly becoming an argument. Erodor flew silently up to her, but she sensed him through Dedira's warning. "They will wish to speak to you soon," he said in his cultured, soft voice. She merely nodded to him, then told Daima. She let Dedira out, and he took to wing after the phoenix. They arrived before the Lords, both phoenix and dragon bowing low to the ground. Yoreh, and his Queen Sadia, looked at the two beings with seemingly infinite wisdom, from their incredibly long lives. "Is this the one you speak of?" Sadia's voice was soft, almost heartbreakingly so. She was not clad in robes or any finery, and the only symbol of her position was a solid gold ring upon her finger, bejeweled and traced with fine lines that made it seemed as if the ring was constantly circling. Yoreh was dressed in a similar outfit to her, a simple jerkin and leggings that were made of rich leather. That seemed the only finery they allowed themselves.

"Ah, Dedira. My child, let her out, please."

Dedira did as he was bid, letting Brenna ascend to light. She looked shaken for a moment, then bowed in the general direction of the Clan Heads present and the Elven Royalty. She felt more than saw the Queen of Elves approach. She daren't meet her eyes. The Queen said, "You wish for us to pardon this one? She is already Naish, should she not be under your jurisdiction by now?"

"Tis . . . complicated," whispered Fafnir, who looked distraught. Graechin looked at them with an annoyed look, showing his distaste at

the 'Half-Breed' being so close to him. The Elven Queen looked at the now straightened girl a moment more before moving back beside her King. They entered into harried and heated conversation for a moment. Then, they both turned to Fafnir.

"This matter is not of importance. What is, however, is our march. Come, we must away to your War Room. A Council of the Mighty must be held!"

Grudgingly, Fafnir bowed her head, turning and leading the Elves and Dwarves and Human Leaders away, into the Mountain that she had claimed. Graechin grinned at Brenna a moment, all teeth and stink, before following.

It took two days at the Council before any of them came out. The Elves, Dwarves, and Men were brought food and drink in that time, while the Clan Heads merely fasted for the time being. When they came out, Brenna, Daima, Reytha, Herold, and several thousand warriors waited with drawn expressions and perked ears. Finally, after what seemed an eternity, the King of Elven-Lands stood. "It is decided: WE MARCH!!!"

Wild cheers echoed to his words. Fafnir looked solemn.

All told, some thirty thousand marched: some fifteen thousands of dwarves, ten thousands of Elves, and five thousands from the Hunter tribes. Besides them, in what one would not call marching, was the beasts of Wold, and several of the forest. Above this great host flew almost a thousand Dragons, and half as many and again of Wyrms. Phoenix's, Eagles, Hippogriffs, and Griffins also flew above and aside to the combined army, peopling the sky with their many, many members. The clan heads strode ahead of them by a few dozen of their powerful strides and strokes, shrunk down to a more reasonable size. All bore a thoughtful expression upon their faces, although what they were for differed.

And, marching astride to this great Army, and yet miles away, was a small, even miniscule group of seven. Daima, Reytha, Brenna, a Wyrm named Rechva, the leopard Julius, a Griffin that would not say his name, and Hunter by the name of Zandwe. All were bound the will of their masters, and they all marched with vigor (or flew, depending). But their missions differed. What they were told publicly: A mission to assassinate the King of all Humans. What really was supposed to happen . . . was far different.

It took two days to reach wherever it was they were supposed to reach in two days (a handy little bit of knowledge, that). Herold was under Fahrirh and his corps. They only tolerated him because he bore the *Asaran-tal*, the mark of the Queen, who was seen as being a patron Saint, of sorts to the Half-Elven. He remembered, a bit sorely, the night before the Great March:

All was a bustle with activity as provisions were made read; water was stored and food prepared for a long journey. Arrows were fletched as a last minute reserve. Herold was loading a large cask of wine onto a wagon. He had no idea where any of his friends. He heard a slight muttering from a little away (you don't get ears like that without some type of boost to your hearing). He finished loading it, and went to investigate.

A few minutes walking and listening later, he found himself inside of a bush. Not just any bush, but one with lots of nice little thorns and stickers. Lovely. Either or, he watched with growing horror this exchange.

"She is not worthy," said the Queen, he normally kind face contorted into a semblance of rage.

Somehow, the Lady Fafnir had used her magics to shrink down to the size of a large Kitsune. Of course, it made sense that she could: being so large would be a bother after a bit. **"Nay, she is not. Please . . . she is precious to my House. Surely, there is a way?"**

"No, my Lady Firedrake. She is raised as a Human, and that is what she will see herself as."

"Stay thy tongue, Youngling. I am stayed myself only for fear of slaying the child. She is precious . . . not only to my House, but to my Children . . . and to me. She is hope in a dark age, where it is hard to find in and of itself. Please . . . I beg of thee . . ." *Both Elf and Half-Elven were struck dumb at her display; surely such a mighty being did not know the meaning of such a small, dishonorable word?*

"I . . . may," said the Queen of the Elven few, after a moment. Softly, she said, *"She must first prove herself, of course."*

"But of course, but of course," *reiterated the Head of Dragon.* **"What must she do?"**

"Destroy that which we dread most."

"Yamaine? Surely you jest? He is guarded by nigh on ten thousand warriors in his capitol alone . . . surely there is but another way?"

"Only if she brings back his head will I grant her my protection. ONLY than," she reaffirmed.

After a moment, **"Fine. But she shall be protected. I will choose her guardians."**

"No. You . . . and Graechin will."

"HE SHALL SLAY HER!!!!" *After a moment, she calmed down. In a deathly quiet voice, she said,* **"If I must. But I will not enjoy this, almost**

as surely as I will regret entering into this arrangement." *Turning on her heels, she left Sadia standing alone in that forsaken ground. Herold left quickly, lest he betray his position.*

After that, he had given Brenna a Kana leaf, showing her one of his own. When she had asked why, he had merely said, "For luck, and protection. It will never die . . . and neither will you, I hope." He wished her luck before joining the march. Some Patron was Sadia, turning down one who could very well be prophecy. Still, he would follow her to death. And, as the immense army of men loomed ever closer, he had the feeling that it wasn't so far off. He clutched the Kana leaf strung round his neck like a totem, silently praying to Gevorh for safety. For him, for Brenna, for each and every one. Gevorh help them.

It took three days to reach High Point. It was, to no one at alls utter surprise, a rather tall mountain. They climbed to the half way point easily, deciding to rest there before continuing onwards. Brenna sat besides her friend, the Kitsune resting lightly beside her on a log while Daima set up tents for them. Being a woman had its perks, Brenna realized a long time ago. "Say, Reytha, why don't you just magic us away to . . . wherever it is we are supposed to go? Seems a lot easier, when I think about it all, instead of all of this walking." The girl was nothing if not blunt.

"'Cause, *Huiliyn*, my Fox-fire can only do so much. Getting all of you lot so far would kill all of us, most likely. Even if it was only one at a time, even. Also, some sort of ancient magic protects Yamaine's yellow ass inside of his capitol, although damned if I know. Still, could we not all use a brisk walk?"

She nodded to Reytha. Brenna looked thoughtful for a moment. "Reytha, what does *Huiliyn* mean? You never answered me the first time around."

Reytha looked stricken for a moment, and then the fox-ish woman coughed into her hand, sounding out something that was akin to "perslagrathma!" Brenna cocked her head to the side in confusion. "Eh?"

"Means 'Darling Child'," called Daima from across the way.

"NOBODY ASKED YOU, SMART ASS!!!!!" Reytha looked down at Brenna from her perch on top of the log, using her abundant tails to support her. "Um . . . cheers?" She offered meekly.

Brenna only shook her head and laughed a little. "I should have expected something like that. I mean, I think you've called me 'dearling' once or twice. No problem . . . *Dal-sata.*"

"Reytha looked surprisedly to her a moment, then shook her head. "'Course, only word of Elvish you can rightly remember, means Mother . . . 'course." Horns sounded in the deep.

The course of the battle that followed was epic in and of itself. Its aftermath even more so. There were one hundred thousand humans, backed up by their cannon and muskets along with archers and footmen. They faced off against forty-thousand opponents, comprising Elves, Dwarves, Men, and the beasts of the Wold. Science versus magic . . . the humans didn't stand a chance.

Herold weaved wildly through the wavering ranks of foot men, sword clashing on armor, and sometimes striking against soft flesh. He felt heady with battle rush, trying not to slip on the gore that reddened the once dusty ground. A river ran red. Said river was a mile away from the immediate battle. The human lines stretched across three miles, and their ranks had stretched some three hundred men back. Of course, no man could fly, and cannon are no good against dragons and wyrms. They were slaughtered.

All was going according to plan-

-Until Graechin decided to launch his attack. Fully half of Wold turned upon itself in a fury so great as to not be seen for a hundred years before or after. Wyrms ganged up to pull dragons out of the sky, phoenix set afire Griffins, Hippogriffs, Eagles, and horses ran rings around the already exhausted Dwarves, who have a deep set, deathly fear of the beasts, set back before Memory.

Only Polious Regla remained true to his word of honor. He had a deep set honor that rivaled that of Dragons, and he saw his folly with casting his lot with the likes of Graechin. He helped Fafnir against her enemies.

But this was more than a battle of men and monsters. Demi-Gods walked the field, bereft of any trappings. They let their true forms loose: deadly, sleek, powerful. Brithal faced off against Kaiden, his manifold tails vainly trying to skewer the Griffin lord in midair. A thousand years of pent up anger and frustrations let itself loose as the combatants battled to a death that was so long in coming. Regla and Lunes gave spirited chase to Sasoran of the Horses, chasing her across the battlefield. They had shrunk down to barely larger than the largest of their kin, for fear of crushing their own underfoot. And, above them, raising a cacophony that drowned out the din of battle, four combatants had taken to flight. Hvarsleg battled against Hyul, Eagle against Phoenix, Flight versus fire, flesh and blood against flame and gentleness.

And, above even them, the air was split by a primal roar as Fafnir and Graechin dueled for supremacy. Only one would survive.

Even before the horns had stopped sounding, the arrows started flying. Arrows are a swordsman's darkest, deepest fear. They cannot be blocked, are hard to dodge, and are used by people who could hide *anywhere* at all on the battlefield, or use their own troops as a shield. As it was, Reytha blasted several out of midair, even catching a couple in her tails to shield Brenna. The Griffin had taken off, and Daima had rolled into the half set up tent, which afforded him some protection. Zandwe, as a big a target as he was, could not dodge in time. Two arrows struck him in the chest, and another scored his arm, runneling his black toned skin with blood. He did not cry out in pain at all, merely grabbed his spear, an immense affair with a dual pointed end used for skewering deer, although it worked just as well on men.

Julius had taken to the bushes before hand to hunt. Rechva merely covered his head with his billowing wings, which were already so pockmarked that a few more holes in them would do nothing to hinder him in any way. The arrows halted after a moment or so.

Then, the war cries were ripped from the throats of a score and a half of cloaked warriors, bearing swords and spears to wound, to kill. Daima smiled grimly.

This was going to be fun. Oh so fun.

"Do you not tire of this game?"

"Never, my Rival. Let us forget our children, our homes in Wold, our Place in the World . . . let us instead looked toward the sun, and let ourselves be lost in the battle-lust. Let us become one.

"United, once again, bound by blood and battle. You are right."

"Just like so many years ago . . . we were comrades once. We were friends. Akin to Brother and Sister. What . . . what happened to them . . . to us?"

"I . . . cannot remember. But, the past is done and dead. You can not change it, so why dwell on it? It can only bring you pain, now."

"Yes . . . Fafnir?"

"Yes?"

"Hold nothing back. If I am to win, then I shall do it at my fullest, as would thee."

"As you will, Graechin, as thou wills it. I shall hold naught back for thee . . . for the old days."

"Aye . . . the olden times. The good times. I shall make sure that, should He see us, He will be proud."

"Oh so proud."
"Let us begin."

Brenna was on her feet, sword drawn, before she knew what was happening. Her body had moved of its own accord, those many hours of drills taking command of her. She blocked a blow from one of their be-hooded attackers. He jumped back, straight into the teeth of Nainya. Daima had opted to sit this one out for now, apparently.

She turned sharply on her heel, bashing her hilt into some ones nose. There was a sharp *crack*, and the sickening sound of blood gushing down. He fell back, clutching at his nose in pain. She didn't pause to see if he was dieing or not; no time for that at all, at the moment. She merely stepped to the next opponent. The Kana leaf Herold had given her was hanging at her neck by a strand of silk, in the fashion of a necklace.

What she did not expect was for three of her enemies to be bowled over, and, in ones case, straight in to the air. Zandwe grinned at her, spear reaching as fast as the lightning to bash the head of one who had managed to struggle up. The three or five arrows sticking out of him in random intervals seemed not to bother him. Still with that sickly grin on his face, he rushed back into battle with the frenzy of one who knew that Death stalked them closely, now. He knew his fate, but fought it even so.

From somewhere in the dark, she heard someone call out, "Get the Forewarned!!!" She felt more than saw the five shadowy enemies rush her. Her sword flashed quickly, and one fell back with a cry, clutching her arm in pain where Brenna had scored her deeply. Her sword was back on guard in an instant; ready to deal death to whomever was fool enough to fight her. It never came to that, however. Out of the billowing darkness (the fire was only smoldering embers by this time) came Daima and Julius. The latter let out an animalistic roar of sheer rage, taking down two of the shadowy figures in a single leap. Daima had his sword drawn faster than the eye could follow. One fell back, headless, while the other matched him blow for blow. After a few strikes back and forth, Daima started to breathe a bit more heavily. Normal people would not have noticed, but, then, Brenna was far from normal. His opponent wasn't either, it seemed, for he pressed his advantage. Daima kicked him in the shin. He hopped on one foot in sheer agony, as Daima's boot had a steel toe. Said Naish relieved his foe of his life, via a blow to the neck.

Brenna saw then that Daima was weaker than she had imagined. He was more for speed and brains to get him through a fight, rather than strength and endurance. It struck her that, maybe, he was the 'better instructor' which Herold had spoken of, so long ago and far away, it seemed. Both man and leopard screamed at her, "Take to the air!!!"

Unconsciously, she released Dedira, and the Dragon had taken to the air before he was even full formed. The wyrm, Rechva, followed closely. Dedira surveyed the battlefield below. Reytha was fighting off enemies from the vantage of a tall rock near the edge of camp. She seemed to fare well versus the abnormally strong and quick foes. Zandwe was rapidly weakening, but still had enough strength to throttle one of the shadowed fighters with his spear, even as others rushed at him. Daima and Julius were circling the dead remains of the campfire. The griffin was nowhere to be seen. **"Alas for us, for we are so few. Rechva, would you aid me?"**

"Nay, firedrake. Your foe is me, and thy doom is nigh."

"What is this treachery?"

"Fool. Would thou believe for but a moment that a race as noble as mine would bow to thy likes? I think no!"

"Fool! Thou knowest not thy folly. I shall end thee here!" The enraged dragon charged at the much larger wyrm, who contemptuously backed away of his attack, sealing his own fate. Dedira spun in midair and blasted him in the back with dragon fire. **"Arrogant fool. I pity thy memory, for surely it will not go well with thee, when Death calls to do Gevorh's bid."** Abruptly, he screeched in pain as the power of a windstorm lashed his back, casting his hide there to ruin. With a screech of triumph, the griffin that had no name came at his. He swatted the small creature with his tail, casting it to the ground, where it bathed in dust and dirt. It groaned once, then lay still. *'Brenna, dearling, I am cast unto ruin. I cannot fly but a little more, enough to reach the ground. My apologies; I was too weak. I fear that this may be my doom.'*

"Stupid overgrown lizard, don't speak like that! We'll . . . we'll get help, yeah, and . . . uh . . ." Dedira merely landed meekly on the ground, casting up a small cloud of dust from his feet. Twenty feet of dragon condensed into the form of a sixteen year old girl . . . no, a woman. Blood was on her blade, even if was not life blood. Even she could tell the Dragon was dieing, and there wasn't a damn thing she could do.

"We are *not* finished with this conversation. Not yet . . ." She trailed off, the battle beckoning her. Daima was slightly limping now, and Julius was scored deeply in his side. There was maybe half of what had started of their enemies, now. One came at her, and she disarmed him with a flick of her wrist. Her training had paid off. Then, three came at her from different sides, all at once. She took the first out with an elbow to the throat, and he gurgled and fell to the ground. The second she scored deeply in her side. She limped off, clutching at the rent. But, the third . . .

It was an accident. He wasn't supposed to shift to the right. Instead of ducking or blocking, he kept his blade lowered. Her slice had the unintended effect of slicing off his head. She stared in horror at the body. That was, until someone came in front of her. Out of instinct she threw her hands up to block the coming blow, although none ever came. Instead, she felt a blade press into her stomach sharply, enough so to draw blood. Her own sword was pressed blunt side to her assailants' neck, completely harmless. She couldn't move it worth a damn. She looked into her eyes . . . And, past those pits of pure dark, her hood was down. Ears tapering to a slight point played shadows with the gently glowing embers of the fire, wind breathing it back life.

"Mother will be pleased," said Eileen

They landed roughly amid the carnage that they had sown. *"Is this what thou wished, Brother?"* They were past the point of pronouns like "He" and "She" and "I". They were now personified simply as "am", simply existing. Bodies surrounded them. Thousands of rent, scored, and pierced bodies . . . tens of thousands. A hundred thousands with enough to spare. Those who survived ran, far and hard. Some might go as far as the Sea of Mar. Elf, Dwarf, Man, Beasts of Wold . . . all fell together.

"No . . . Sister, this . . . is . . . is . . ."

"Our doom. Do you believe for a second that He would be pleased?"

"But . . . the Prophecy . . ."

"Even that which is set in stone was carved out of the living rock to begin with. Prophecy hath led thou astray, Brother."

"Sister . . . I believe that, now, we have . . . done all we could. Our Children will go on . . . Hopefully. But . . . we have caused this, and we may do so again." "Their Brethren around them nodded in agreement, sporting their wounds with pride.

"Let us . . . go to Father. He will be oh so proud of us, now . . . even after . . . this . . ." The Dragon trailed off. Soundlessly, all twelve of them let the night take them away, unto the Heavens.

YES, MY CHILDREN . . . I AM OH SO PROUD OF YOU ALL.

"Let go. You cannot win against us. Your bastard friends . . . they would betray you long before you could reach him. Just let what will be, be." She was insufferably smug looking. Brenna fumed at her.

"You know, I am starting to hate Destiny."

"Stone will weather, but it will not break to the wind or will of anything."

"Still, I could find a very big mallet, see if I don't!"

"You are amusing. But Mother wishes to see you, Young One."

"Who is this Mother that you go on about?"

"She has a name, you know." Eileen seemed to be caught up in some memories. "Some call her . . . Mab. It is an ugly name, for one such as she. I don't like it at all." She sounded like a child to Brenna.

"Sounds like a right old Bitch." You could hear the capitol letter.

"Shut up! She is Beautiful and Graceful and Everything that me and you could never hope to be! I would *die* for her!"

Brenna cast a quick look about. Zandwe was dead, and Julius looked just about. Daima was fending off half a dozen men alone, as was Reytha. Her two friends were going to die. Her head snapped back to Eileen angrily, face contorting in rage.

"Well, guess what? My friends are better than that wench, and I would die for *them*. And you know what?" She pushed herself onto Eileen's blade, ignoring the pain that clouded her vision and the blood in her mouth. "I'm a lot more suicidal than you, bitch!" Her blade twisted in her grasp, and she pulled with the last of her failing strength. Eileen fell to the floor, while her head stopped a few feet away. A shadow escaped from her like a poison, the vapor casting itself at Brenna. She did nothing to stop it. *'I guess that . . . I wasn't strong enough.'* The blade felt jagged inside of her. The Half-Elves who attacked withdrew in disarray.

"Nay, 'twas I. If only I had been older, stronger, faster. If only—"

'Ah, shut it, would ya? 'm sleepy . . . tired. Dedira?"

"Yes, Dear Heart?"

'Is it nice . . . up there?' They both knew where she meant.

"Yes, Love. I will show you . . . someday. But . . . the Other World calls us. Let us not tarry." She mumbled something incoherently, only half surprised to see the shadow go into her. No . . . it was drawn like a charm to the Kana leaf hung about her neck. The leaf wilted.

"Well . . . that's a . . . surprise." She felt Reytha skid to a stop next to her, and Daima behind. Julius was dead, but not before three more Half-Elves had fallen to his claws and teeth, throats rent and ruined.

"It's . . . nothing at all, Deary. We'll . . . have you fixed up in—"

"Don' . . . don't give me that . . . bull . . ." Brenna held up a hand shakily. "I can't be saved now, I remember that much. And . . . I, we, wanna go . . . You gotta . . . forget that I was ever . . . here . . ."

She cradled her head in her arms, tears falling down her classical face. "I could never do that . . . My Kit."

"Mom . . . You gotta let a girl grow up a bit, ya? I . . . wanna see the world a bit. I wanna . . . fly. Like Dedira. It'll be . . . alright." Reytha and

Daima felt so helpless now. She kissed the dieing girls brow. Daima idly noted that the starting's of a ninth tail were already starting to grow in. So, Reytha's greatest fear was letting go of what she loved. Figures.

The girls' eyes clouded over, and Reytha spilled more tears. Silently, Daima placed the spell on her. Her body faded into the night, leaving only the bloodstained sword and the withered Kana leaf. Daima picked the wilted parody up. He stood, the weeping Kitsune still cradling the space where her pseudo-daughters head used to be. A parody of an Angel. "Reytha?"

"Yes?"

"Let's get him. We got some business to finish before we rest." The two set off into the darkening night.

Two days later, Herold watched as they came back. They cast the head of Yamaine in front of the Elf Queen contemptuously. She cast her gaze over it, then over the two battered, tired warriors in front of her. She turned around, robes fluttering in the slight breeze. As one already dead, Daima went over to the stunned Herold. He lightly pressed the withered Kana leaf into his hand. The Half-Elf shook his head in bewilderment. They paid him no heed. The two wandered to the edge of the battle. Bodies littered the field; man, dwarf, elf, half-elf . . . all bound by blood, battle . . . and death. The stench was almost unbearable, but they ignored it.

When they got to the edge, Reytha looked him in the eye. Startling yellow eyes gazed back at her solemnly. After Brenna died, they had lost the spark that had animated them. But, then, so had hers. "Daima?"

"Yeah?" His voice was hoarse from yelling.

"Do you think that . . . it's hopeless? Us staying to fight her."

"Brenna said it would be alright . . . and we believe her."

"I guess . . . do you trust her?"

"To the ends of the Earth." He smiled slightly.

She smiled slightly back at him. "I think I'll go for a run."

"Reytha?"

"Yeah?"

"Mind if we join you?" He had stopped using "I" when Brenna died, and not just for Nainya. He was living three lives now, one for him, another for Dedira, and one for Brenna.

"I would like that." The two were surrounded in a pure white light, and, when it cleared, a nine tailed fox and a wolf sped off, side by side, the sun beating down on their backs. A Phoenix cried out heartbreakingly as they sped onward, bathed in dust and dawn.

I AM SO PROUD OF YOU ALL . . . MY CHILDREN . . .

Printed in the United States
78159LV00003B/282

9 781425 752231